This book is one of the best I have read, the honesty, love, laughter and tears all captured in one brilliant read.

An excellent read! Touching, humorous, loving, it describes what only those parents closely associated with autism go through. For those of us who are not familiar with autism, it was an eye-opener in showing the stresses and strains, but also the love and rewards that can come with it.

It is full of honesty, humour but most of all love and respect with seemingly getting little in return. Everyone should read this book, whether touched by autism or not. It would help to make us all more tolerant and accepting of those that are a little bit different.

I loved this book! As a parent of two autistic people myself, I can assure would be readers that the life described by Denis Deasy in this entertaining tale is spot on!

Amazon reviews for
'I'm Sorry, My Son's Autistic'

What an amazing follow up to 'Living in Harry's World' joining Harry and his dad on a heart-warming but rollercoaster of a ride into adulthood. The author really opened my eyes to the world of autism and is a very humbling read. Fantastic read that I couldn't put down. I can't wait until the next instalment.

Author Denis Deasy brilliantly conveys the pressures of dealing with stressful behavioural issues by injecting a degree of humour which is not only entertaining but also gives the reader some insights into the realities of living with autism. I laughed out loud at times and had a tear in my eye at others. This follow-up is highly recommended.

The relationship between Harry and his father is so moving. I loved the many funny incidents and anecdotes - based on Harry's view of the world. A very honest, yet uplifting, account of life with an autistic teenager.

Amazon reviews for 'From This Day Forward'

The final part of the trilogy from author Denis Deasy concludes the story arc of autistic Harry and his long suffering father. Beautifully written, we see Harry at 30 in a relationship and planning to marry Bernadette. Just like the previous two books in the series, you'll laugh out loud at some parts and will have tears in your eyes at others. Books like this really do give an insight into life with autism but few do it as well as Deasy.

The completion of the 'Harry' trilogy and the best yet? Charming, insightful and full of humour. These books have offered real insight into families living with autism and yet manage to both entertain and educate the casual reader. Highly recommended!

Having read this third book about Harry, getting more insight into the world of an autistic person, the heartache, and sometimes joy, of the parents involved, I am still in awe, and have full respect for them, for dealing with, and working through a life-long commitment.

Don't Lick
The Mailbox

Denis Deasy

Grosvenor House
Publishing Limited

This book is published by
Grosvenor House Publishing Ltd
Link House
140 The Broadway, Tolworth, Surrey, KT6 7HT.
www.grosvenorhousepublishing.co.uk

This book is a work of fiction. Any resemblance to
people or events, past or present, is purely coincidental.

A CIP record for this book
is available from the British Library

ISBN 978-1-80381-260-1
eBooks ISBN 978-1-80381-261-8

Dedication

This book is dedicated to Tony Prouse and
Joanna Rees.
Thank you for all the time you spent on my book
and for your friendship and kindness.

Acknowledgements

Thanks to:

Sean Poole for your positive and enthusiastic comments throughout the whole process of writing this book.

My lifelong friend, Tony, for his amazing editing skills and perceptive notations.

Joanna Rees, who continues to believe in me and taking the time once again to share her most valued observations.

Joanmarie – I am so extremely proud that your art work is the first thing the readers will see when they pick up my book. And thanks for the inspired book title.

Prologue

'Are you having an affair?' I ask my wife.

She looks at me for what seems like an eternity and nods.

'Is it Rob?'

'Yes. I'm so sorry, Danny.'

'How long has this been going on?'

'Nearly six months.'

'Fucking hell, Karen.'

'I've hardly seen you these past few months. You've either been at work or going to conferences all around the country.'

'Don't blame me for trying to get that promotion. I did it for us.'

She doesn't respond.

'Come on, tell me all the gory details. When did you first have sex?'

'Let's not get into that right now.'

'I hate to disagree but I need to know everything,' I shout at her.

She slumps onto the sofa.

'I'll find out sooner or later so just put me out of my misery.'

'It was the weekend you went to Leeds.'

She puts her head in her hands and stares at the floor.

'Have the decency to look at me for fucks sake.'

'He came to return your books. We got chatting, had too much wine and …'

'Screwed each other,' I scream at her.

She nods.

'In our bed?'

She doesn't reply which is all I need to know.

'I can't believe what I'm hearing. I know that we haven't been getting on recently but I never thought you'd cheat on me. I can't get my head around it.'

'We haven't had sex for ages. We're drifting apart.'

'I've been under a lot of pressure at work, you know that. That's hardly an excuse to jump into bed with one of my so called friends after a couple of glasses of wine.'

'There's something else.'

I look nervously at her. What could she possibly say that will make me feel worse than I do right now?

'I'm pregnant.'

CHAPTER ONE:
TWELVE YEARS LATER

'One for the road?' I ask Maria.

'Yeah, why not? No work tomorrow.'

I work in IT for a company called *FixIT* and these past few weeks we've been working really hard implementing changes for a retail company to get the new software deployed in time for their peak Christmas period. Today was the deadline and we made it by the skin of our teeth, as my mother used to say. Maria is an IT colleague. Tonight is the office Christmas party. *FixIT* has gone to the great expense of booking a dingy-looking room in a pub very close to our office. They have also splashed out on cold sausage rolls accompanied by the usual triangle sandwiches where I have to organise a search party to locate a piece of ham. The Michelin standard food is completed by pineapple and cheese on sticks. If it wasn't for Maria I would've headed straight home. Watching *Pointless* is fractionally preferable to hanging out with IT nerds.

'So what are your plans for Christmas?' I ask as I hand Maria a glass of wine.

'I'm going to my parents on Christmas Day and the rest of the time I'm just chilling. I need the rest.'

'Tell me about it. It's been a crazy time at work.'

'And how are you spending Christmas?' She asks.

'My parents are both deceased. I've no brothers or sisters so I'll be just sitting in front of the box watching Morecombe and Wise episodes that are probably around fifty years old.'

'That sounds a bit sad.'

'I've been living on my own now for quite a while so it's not much different from most weekends.'

'How long have you been divorced if you don't mind me asking?'

'It'll be eleven years in March.'

'Wow, that long. You've never met anybody special since then?'

'No, I'm afraid not, but to be honest I haven't really dated much. I've got used to being on my own, although that's not really a good thing.'

'Why did you get divorced? I'm sorry, I shouldn't have asked you that, I've had too much to drink.'

'It's not a problem but where do I start? I dated Karen for two years before I popped the question. We were both twenty-three when we got married. The first few years were great, we did everything together but then I got my first IT job and I found it very difficult to keep up with everything which stressed me out. I suppose my anxiety affected my relationship with her. However, after a while I got the hang of things and then worked all the hours God sent to try and get a promotion. This involved going all around the country deploying software to our clients and attending conferences, you know the score. When I was at home she seemed very distant. I just knew something was wrong so when I eventually confronted her she admitted to having an affair with a guy who happened to be one of my friends.'

'That's awful.'

'I was so angry. We had a massive argument and I packed my bags that same night and left. I haven't seen her since.'

'Didn't you come into contact with her during the divorce?'

'No, my lawyer took care of everything.'

'I didn't know any of that.'

'Not many people do. I don't talk about it much,' I reply before taking a sip of my beer.

'But that's not all. She then told me that she was pregnant.'

'With his child?'

'Oh yeah. We started trying for a baby a couple of years before that but nothing happened. We then had tests and I found out that I've got a very low sperm count. We were thinking of trying IVF but it's so expensive and we just weren't in a financial position to pursue that. Anyway, she told me straight away I wasn't the father.'

'When you left that night did she try to stop you?'

'Yes she did but I knew the marriage was dead. The trust had gone.'

'How did you cope?'

'I was devastated, although it took some time to realise it wasn't entirely her fault. I played my part.'

'What do you mean?'

'I was just so ambitious with work. I never turned down any assignment regardless of how long I'd be away from home. I was too focused to notice the impact it had on my relationship until it was too late.'

'Did she talk to you about your work commitments?'

'Yes, but I just thought that she was over exaggerating, having a bit of a moan. I remember telling her that she would thank me when we move into a bigger house in a nicer area.'

'So what made you suspect she was cheating on you?'

'Wherever I was away I'd always ring her in the evening and her mobile was either engaged or there was no answer. Then one weekend one of our nosey neighbours told me that they'd seen my friend Rob come to my house a few times a week while I was away. Karen or Rob never mentioned any of this to me so I became suspicious. I asked the neighbour to text me whenever she noticed Rob coming around and I'd ring Karen then. The times she did answer she mostly told me that she was doing household chores or watching TV. It didn't take a rocket scientist to work out what was going on.'

'Did she try to contact you after you left?'

'Yeah, she texted a lot but I didn't respond. She was dead to me and it certainly felt like grieving at the time.'

'Any contact with Rob?'

'No, but I wanted to beat the shit out of him so many times.'

'Again, I'm sorry for bringing this up, we're supposed to be celebrating.'

'There's no need to apologise, it happened so long ago. I haven't talked about Karen for many years. It actually feels good.'

'Then maybe we should do this more often,' Maria looks at me intently.

'Yes, we should.'

Half an hour later we both leave the pub. Maria heads towards Waterloo overground station while I get on the tube. Was she actually flirting with me earlier by suggesting that we should socialise again? Maybe it was just the drink clouding my judgement.

My thoughts turn to Karen. From time to time I do wonder what her life is like now, after all I did spend seven years with her. Is she still with Rob? I did find out that she had a boy. He must be eleven years old now. Does she ever think of me? Does she regret sleeping with Rob?

I'll probably never find out.

CHAPTER TWO

It's a cold, frosty Christmas Day. From my kitchen window I see a family walking past. The two children look excited as they clutch their toys. It's a happy scene. As usual there are no Christmas presents for me to open. My only present this year was from a secret Santa at work which was *Showaddywaddys Greatest Hits*. Why on earth would anyone think that I like Showaddywaddy? Unless it was a joke, but I don't think so as my IT colleagues have yet to discover a sense of humour. I gave it to Cancer Research. It should fetch at least a quid and I feel good that I've done my bit for charity for the year. The last decent Christmas present I received was five years ago and it was a laptop. It was from my mother who passed away suddenly on Boxing Day.

Until then I used to love Christmas. When I was growing up some of our relatives would come over on Christmas Day and it always turned into a sing song. Lovely memories. Even after I got married I always had my parents over on Christmas Day. They really liked Karen and were distraught when our marriage ended. For a long time my mum begged me to contact Karen but she eventually got the message that was never going to happen. I haven't even put up a Christmas tree this year. What's the point?

I make myself another cup of tea and settle in front of the television to watch the same old festive repeats. Although I will watch the Queens speech. As a young kid my father told me to pay attention during Her Majesty's broadcasts. 'That lady talks a lot of sense and she'll steer you along the right path in life,' he would say.

'But I bet she doesn't do any hoovering,' my mum always replied.

'There's 775 rooms in Buckingham Palace. You can't expect the Queen to do all of them,' was my father's response.

'A couple wouldn't go amiss.'

You'd think that this was a light hearted conversation; it wasn't.

After the Queen's speech I'll crack open my £9.99 bottle of sparkling wine and fall to sleep in front of the TV. Maybe Maria was right, it is all rather sad. Three minutes into the *Strictly Come Dancing Christmas Special* and I'm already bored so I boot up my laptop. When I log onto Facebook I notice there's a message waiting for me. When I open it I can't believe what's in front of me.

'Remember me? It's been a while. How have you been? I hope you are well and having a fabulous day. You always loved Christmas. Let me know how you're getting on. Take care, Karen.'

I read it several times as it seems surreal to me. For years after our split I felt extremely bitter towards her at the way our marriage ended but more recently that has diminished and now I'm at the stage where I rarely think of Karen, apart from the other night when Maria asked about my divorce. To see this message just blows my mind.

With apologies to Her Majesty I crack open the wine and before I know it I've drunk three quarters of the bottle while staring at the message.

It's been over a decade since our last and rather heated conversation. Why is she suddenly contacting me? Has something happened to her to prompt this? There's only one way to find out. I take another gulp of wine before I start typing.

'To say I'm shocked to hear from you is an understatement. Is everything OK?'

I wait anxiously for over half an hour before a reply appears.

'Can we meet sometime next week? I'll perfectly understand if you don't want to.'

'Why do you want to meet?'

'I want to explain some things to you.'

'After all this time?'

'It'll be much easier if we can meet up rather than messaging each other.'

'OK, why not?'

'Is tomorrow too soon?'

'No, it's fine.'

'Can you come over at midday?'

'Yes, are you still at our… I mean your house?'

'Yeah, still here.'

'OK, I'll see you tomorrow.'

'Great, enjoy the rest of your Christmas Day.'

CHAPTER THREE

I wake up with a slight hangover as I continued drinking after the online conversation.

It's hard to believe that I'll be seeing Karen again today, but I'm now wondering if Rob will also be there. That'll be awkward at best and likely confrontational but would Karen invite me over in these circumstances?

I hold that bastard equally responsible for the break-up of my marriage and to this day I feel a little ashamed that I never took him to task. Rob and I were in the same class throughout our school years. Even back then he was a bit of a know it all but that always seemed to work in his favour with the females as he inevitably went out with the prettiest girls and that continued into his twenties. He didn't want to settle down, he just wanted to have fun and I reluctantly admired him for that. He was certainly a larger than life character – a completely different personality to me. However, he got bored easily and broke many hearts along the way. He wasn't academically clever and I used to go to his house to help him with his maths homework even though he showed no interest. Most of the time he just told me to write down the answers which I did. How naïve and stupid was I? When Rob inevitably failed all his exams he simply worked for his father who owned his own building company. Again, everything fell into place for him.

Karen and I bought the two bedroom house in Brixton soon after we got married. It's just off the high street and very near the tube station – a great location. However, we never planned to stay there long term. We both wanted to move further out to a bigger house in preparation for starting a family. As part of the divorce settlement Karen kept the house but I was paid a lump sum for my half of the mortgage. I used this to put a down payment on my extremely small two bedroom house in Vauxhall, which is only two stops on the underground from Brixton. I never did make it out to the suburbs.

As I walk along the familiar Brixton streets, memories of our early life together come flooding back. I'm surprised to see many of the same shops still here – the newsagents, the Post Office, the launderette... it feels strangely re-assuring. I walk past the Prince of Wales pub where we spent many happy evenings and I'm tempted to pop in for a quick pint to steady my nerves but decide against it.

I eventually arrive at the house that I lived in for over five years. The matchbox garden looks in better condition than I remember but that's not hard as I hate gardening and always used my bad back as an excuse not to get involved.

As I stare at the front of the house I'm beginning to regret coming. Why did I agree to this without thinking it through?

But before I have any chance to change my mind, the front door opens and Karen steps out.

It's like time has stood still as she looks the same, perhaps with a few more flecks of grey in her long blonde hair. She remains slim and her blue eyes are still stunning.

She smiles and embraces me, which takes me by surprise.

'How are you doing? You look great,' she says.

'I'm OK,' is all I can say.

'Come in,' she says and leads me into her house.

As I enter the living-room I can see straight away the differences since I last was here. Not surprisingly the wallpaper, carpet and sofa are different but my book shelves are still standing, which, given the fact that I failed my Woodwork 'O' level, is amazing.

'It feels pretty strange being back here.'

'I can imagine. Now what are you having to drink? I have Carlsberg.'

'You remembered.'

She nods.

'Yes, thank you.'

She returns with my drink and she's holding a glass of white wine.

'Well I hope you had a nice Christmas,' she says as she holds up her glass.

'Ditto,' I reply, resisting the temptation to clink her glass before we both take a sip of our drinks.

'If you told me yesterday that I'd be sitting in this room…'

'I can't tell you how many times I've wanted to contact you.'

'So why now?'

'I've never forgiven myself for what happened to us. I know I blamed the fact that you were away so much but that doesn't excuse what I did.'

'Karen, there's no need to explain. I no longer hold any bad feeling towards you. It happened so long ago and we've both moved on.' Although if I'm truthful I would like some clarification on why she had it off with one of my best friends.

'Have you remarried?' She asks.

'No.'

After all this time there's no embarrassing silences, we've just carried on as if we had only spoken to each other yesterday. But Karen was always honest, others would say blunt even, until the last few weeks of our marriage that is.

'Are you in a relationship now?' She asks.

'How about asking me if I still have Corn Flakes for breakfast instead? Let's take it one step at a time.'

'I'm sorry, I'm really nervous.'

'You and me both.'

'So do you?' She asks.

'Do what?'

'Still have Corn Flakes every morning?'

'Yes.'

She smiles and takes another sip of her wine.

'It's time for me to ask you a question,' I say.

'Go for it.'

'Where's Rob?'

'We got divorced six months ago.'

'Oh, I'm sorry to hear that,' I say trying to sound convincing.

'Liar,' she replies, smiling.

'Did I hate him for sleeping with you? Of course I did, but I don't wish you unhappiness, not now anyway. So what happened?'

'The first couple of years were fine but he got restless and started going out with his friends more and more. I suspected that he was seeing women and on a few occasions I confronted him but he kept on denying it, so as a last resort I contacted a detective agency.'

'I thought that only happened in films.'

'Believe me it's real and very costly but it served its purpose. They followed him for a month and caught him with two women. When I accused him again he told me that I was paranoid but after I showed him the photos his face went white. For once I was one step ahead of him. I had already packed his bags and he left that night.'

'Wow, how are you coping?'

'I'm doing OK. It's actually a relief not worrying where he is and who he's with. To be honest, Danny I've been thinking more and more about us recently and how I let you down. I just wanted to meet you and apologise, albeit a decade too late.'

'Karen, please don't carry that guilt, life's too short. I don't hate you, if I did, would I be here today?'

'There's no ulterior motive. I'm not trying to get us back together or want anything from you, I would like us to be friends again and if we have no further contact after today then at least we can end it all amicably and that'll please me more than you could ever know. There's another reason why I asked you here, since Rob left I've had a clear out and there's some stuff of yours in the loft. Do you mind having a look and just take anything you want?'

'Yeah, no problem. Do you want me to do that now?'

'There's no rush.'

'There's one thing you haven't mentioned.'

'What's that?'

'Your son.'

'How did you know?'

'I stayed friends with Alex and Colin for a short while. They told me.'

'His name is Sam, he's eleven years old and he's autistic.'

'Where is he now?'

'He's with Belinda. She's going to New York tomorrow for two weeks and wanted to spend time with Sam before she went. She's very close to him.'

Belinda is Karen's sister.

'Does he speak?'

'Yes, he has Aspergers which is on the more able end of the autistic spectrum.'

'I really don't know much about autism I'm afraid, although I do remember watching that Dustin Hoffman film.'

'*Rain Man*.'

'That's it.'

'The media tend to portray autistic people as being supremely talented at something just like Dustin Hoffman's character in that film. The reality is very different.'

'When did you realise he was autistic?'

'His language wasn't great and when we had gatherings with family and friends I noticed how much more advanced his peers were. Not only verbally but much better able to communicate.'

'What age was Sam then?'

'Two.'

'Did you talk to any of his teachers?'

'Yes but they just told me that kids all develop at their own pace. They were confident that he would catch up.'

'How are his language skills now?'

'Much better but that hides loads of issues which I don't really want to get into right now.'

'Is he is at a special school?'

'Yes. He was diagnosed a few weeks before his fourth birthday and then went to a SLD pre-school. He's now in an autistic school not far from here.'

'What's SLD?'

'Severe Learning Difficulty. I'm sorry I should've explained.'

'I had no idea about any of this. How did Rob cope with it?'

'He didn't accept the autism diagnosis and kept saying that he'll grow out of it. I remember telling him so many times to face up to the truth but I don't think he ever did.'

'How does he get on with Sam?'

'When Sam was very young Rob mentioned to me that he was looking forward to the day when he could take his son down to his local for a pint and also go to see Chelsea play but he must have realised at some point that this was never going to happen, not in the way he envisaged anyway. He then distanced himself from Sam and that was heartbreaking.'

'Does he see him now?'

'Once a month at best and even then he just takes him to the local park and is usually back within half an hour.'

She takes another sip of her wine.

'I didn't drag you here on Boxing Day to offload my problems, I just wanted to see you and make amends for a mistake that I made a long time ago.'

'Please don't beat yourself up about it.'

'But still, I'd like to explain...'

'There's no need, you've enough to deal with right now. Anyway I better get going.'

'Thanks for coming over at such short notice, Danny. I know it couldn't have been easy for you.'

'I'm glad you contacted me, Karen. Rest assured I'll be back to clear out my stuff from the loft.'

We hug each other awkwardly before I leave and make my way to the tube station.

When I arrive home I reflect on my time with Karen. I wasn't too surprised about her being divorced from Rob. It was always obvious to me that he couldn't commit to a long-term relationship even given the fact that he has a son. To find out that Sam is autistic was sad news and it was distressing to hear that Rob's involvement with his son is virtually non-existent. Life must be tough for Karen right now.

I was prepared to question her on the affair but after hearing her news about Sam it didn't seem right. I actually left pretty sharpish as I was somewhat anxious about meeting Sam. What would I say to an autistic eleven-year-old boy? Because I'm an only child I have no nieces or nephews so I've had zero interaction with children.

As I feel bad for leaving so early, I log onto Facebook and start typing a message to Karen.

'Great catching up with you today. Would definitely like to see you again.'

Ten minutes later comes the reply.

'Thanks again for coming over. I wanted to say more about what happened between us. How about coming over on Saturday? There's still a few cans of Carlsberg in the fridge and the stairs to the loft are now a lot safer than when you last climbed them.'

'OK, sounds good. The same time?'

'Yeah, that's fine. Some of the anxiety that I've carried for such a long time already feels a little lighter. Thank you.'

'Glad I could help.'

'And I can't wait for you to meet my son.'

CHAPTER FOUR

The last forty-eight hours have been so surreal. I'm still in a state of disbelief as I had never expected to see Karen again.

It would have been easier to ignore her Christmas Day message but I would have been forever wondering why she had made contact after all this time. To some extent I still am. Perhaps she does only want to make amends and nothing else. I'd like to think so. But its gone up another level with the prospect of meeting Sam. Why am I so nervous? Is it because of his autism or the fact that he's a symbol of why our marriage ended? Would I have stayed with her if she wasn't pregnant? I don't think so but that was definitely a deal breaker.

The fact that he's Rob's son also doesn't sit well with me.

However it was me who messaged her first after our meeting and suggested that we should see each other again. I just didn't expect it to happen so soon.

Last night I did look at numerous autism articles on the internet but it covers such a broad range of behaviours that it's difficult to judge where Sam fits into it.

My time with Karen was very pleasant but was I too nice to her given the fact that she betrayed me so cruelly? I wouldn't quite say that she ruined my life but she certainly changed it forever. It took another five years before I went on an online date. That didn't work out and neither did subsequent ones. Perhaps she instilled in me an underlying distrust of women. Why didn't I say that to her?

All these thoughts are still with me as I walk familiar Brixton streets again and before I know it I'm standing in front of her house.

I ring the door bell and a young boy answers it. He looks just like Karen, small, slim with fair hair and blue eyes. He even has that same bemused expression that I recognise in his mother. He must be Sam.

'And who the hell are you?' He asks.

'I'm Danny, a friend of your mums. Is she in?'

'Where do you live?'

'Vauxhall.'

'That's on the Victoria line and it has a big Sainsbury's.'

'That's right.'

'Do they sell Anchor butter in that Sainsbury's?'

'I don't know but I presume they do.'

'Why don't you know that?'

'I don't eat Anchor butter.'

'That's a bit crazy. What butter do you eat?'

'I prefer margarine.'

'Only confused people like margarine, I think you can disappear now,' Sam replies before very calmly shutting the door.

I stand there for a couple of minutes, not sure whether to ring the bell again. Finally Karen opens the door.

'I'm so sorry, Danny, I was in the toilet. You've met Sam then?'

'Yes, we had a butter and margarine conversation.'

'As you do. Please come in.'

We enter the living-room where Sam is sitting in an armchair just staring at the opposite wall. I look over at the wall to see if there's anything interesting but it's just a plain wall.

'Sam, this is Danny. He's an old friend.'

Sam is still fixated on the wall.

'Sam, don't be so rude. Say hello to Danny.'

'I don't like margarine people. They make me feel queasy.'

'Danny, how about you get rid of all your margarine tubs and buy Anchor butter instead?' Karen asks me, adding a wink.

'That's a good idea. It's Anchor for me from now on.'

I thought that this would get a reaction but no.

'What football team do you support?' I ask Sam.

'Chelsea.'

'Who's your favourite player?'

'I don't know any of the footballers' names. I just like the hot dogs at Stamford Bridge, especially when they put onions and tomato ketchup on it. I always bring my own plate with me to stop any of the onions falling onto the ground.'

'That's very wise.'

'Do you like doors?' He asks.

'What do you mean?'

'The rectangle doors that you pass through every day, do you like them?'

'They're OK.'

'So you don't actually give a shit about them?'

'No, I think they're fine,' I reply, not wanting to upset him.

'It makes me cry if anyone slams doors.'

'He has a thing about doors,' Karen whispers to me. I nod in return as if I understand; I don't.

'But I always shut them quietly so it's all good, OK?' Karen tells her son.

'I suppose so.'

'Why don't you tell Danny about your hobbies?'

'I like playing with ants. They're a great laugh.'

'Danny and I were actually married a long time ago,' Karen says nervously.

'Does that mean I have two fathers?'

'No, Danny was married to me before you were born but we broke up before I met your father.'

Karen avoids my look at her after that lie.

'But where's Dad? I haven't seen him in six weeks and four days. He never replies to my texts.'

'He's busy, Sam, but I'll try to get him to come over and see you.'

If he's not too busy frolicking around with numerous women.

'Danny and I want to have a chat so why don't you go to your bedroom and watch TV?'

'It was nice meeting you, Sam.'

He stands up and stares at me for what seems like ages. He then leaves without saying anything.

'Social niceties are not his strength,' Karen tells me.

I smile at her.

'Carlsberg?'

'Yes please,' I reply a little too quickly. 'On second thoughts, can I just pop up to the loft first?'

'Of course.'

'Is the ladder still in the same place?'

'Yes, we've got a new one, Rob fell off it.'

'Nothing broken I hope?'

'Unfortunately only the ladder.'

As I position the ladder, Sam ventures onto the landing.

'Everything OK?' I ask.

'The metal ladder is strong but I reckon if you fall off it you'll probably die, so I just want to see if you make it up there alive.'

'To make it more secure can you hold it for me?'

'No way, I don't want your arse falling on my head.'

'OK, fair enough,' I reply.

Under Sam's watchful eye I make it up to the loft without dying.

The last time I was up here most of the flooring wasn't secure and I had to mostly walk on the beams but not now. It looks like the sort of place to get away from it all; very cosy.

I spot a few boxes with my name written on them. I open the first one and it's full of football medals and trophies. I was captain of a five-a-side team and we were very successful. Although I haven't thought about those days in so many years I suddenly miss the guys I used to play with – Tony, Steve, Mickey and Ray. We had such a bond. Such carefree days. I wonder what they're doing now? Probably married with kids. How did I ever lose touch with them? I suppose life takes over.

The next couple of boxes have my clothes in them. I left the house in such a hurry on that fateful night that I only threw a handful of clothes into a suitcase and just couldn't face going back to the house to pick up the rest. Although I'm still slim I don't think the trousers will fit me so these will be going to charity or maybe the local dump. I am surprised that Karen hadn't deposed of them.

Another unmarked box contains our wedding album. I haven't got any photos from that day and obviously haven't seen this album in so many years. It still looks in pristine condition. Wow, we look so young and happy. The future looked so hopeful on that day. Sometimes when I recall events of the past I didn't realise how happy I was at the time but on my wedding day I knew that it was the happiest I've ever felt. I had married the person I loved the most and was surrounded by all the people closest to me.

A tear trickles down my face as I recall what happened a few years later.

I'm assuming that Karen wants to keep the album, which touches me.

There's more photos in the box – most of them include Karen and me on holidays in New York, Paris and one great trip to Scarborough. Such wonderful memories that I've mostly forgotten or subconsciously blocked.

The trip back down the ladder carrying the boxes was somewhat scary. The ladder is at a forty-five degree angle directly overlooking the stairs. There's no room for error.

'I think I'll have that beer now,' I say as I enter the living-room.

Soon afterwards she hands me a can.

'I see you've brought down your clothes,' Karen says.

'Yes, I'm surprised you kept them.'

'I always thought that one day you'd come back for them.'

A few moments of embarrassing silence follows.

'So what do you think of Sam? Be honest.' Karen says.

'He's very different to anyone I've ever met. I can't read him at all. Does he have any friends?'

'Only his class mates. He has no non-autistic friends. Without wishing to be the prophet of doom I think that'll always be the case. It's hard enough for adults to understand him, for normal children it's just impossible.'

'That must be so difficult for you.'

'Do I wish Sam was not autistic? Of course I do, but it isn't going to change so I just get on with it; I've no choice. When I go to a restaurant or a pub and I see other kids his age really acting up and Sam is just sitting there reading a book, I do feel like saying something to the parents as it pisses me off but of course I never do. I don't underestimate the problems of bringing up non-autistic children but you have to multiply that stress level many times when you're dealing with autism. It's as simple as that.'

'Did you want another child?'

'Initially I did but Rob wasn't keen. When we found out about Sam that made the decision for me. There was a realistic chance that the next child could also be autistic and I just couldn't face it again. I know that sounds awful but...'

'It's perfectly understandable,' I say.

Loud knocking on the front door interrupts our conversation. Karen dashes to the hallway presumably to answer it before Sam gets upset as he doesn't seem to cope with loud noises.

'Rob, what are you doing here?'

'It didn't take him long to get his feet under the table, did it? Where is he?'

In a few seconds it looks like I'm finally going to get reacquainted with the man who destroyed my marriage.

CHAPTER FIVE

'So how long have you two been back together?' Rob asks as he enters the living-room.

'It's none of your business and thanks for nearly breaking the door down. You know how that upsets Sam,' Karen tells her ex-husband. Rob doesn't respond and just stares at me.

'By the way, why haven't you seen your son in weeks?' She asks.

'I've been busy at work but I'm here now, aren't I?'

'Only because of Danny.'

Suddenly there's a loud thumping from upstairs.

'Now look what you've done! Seeing as you're now suddenly the best father in South London, do you want to go upstairs and calm your son down?'

Rob doesn't reply.

'I thought not,' Karen replies before rushing out of the living-room.

'So you're after my sloppy seconds?' Rob asks me.

Although the tone of his voice is slow and measured I can tell he's hiding a lot of anger.

'You always did have a way with words,' I reply, although I'm disgusted with his disrespectful reference to Karen.

There's an awkwardness between us. Given Sam's distressed state I don't want to antagonize Rob anymore right now, but there's an awful lot I'd like to say to him. That can wait for another day.

'You never remarried then?' He asks with a smirk.

I know exactly what that smirk means – that I haven't recovered from the breakdown of my marriage but I don't rise to the bait.

'I was surprised you didn't pay me a visit after you found out about me and Karen,' he adds.

'There were a couple of times when I did go to your house but you weren't in. In retrospect that was a good thing because I could've got into a lot of trouble. I wouldn't have been in control of my actions.'

'Yeah right,' he laughs.

I feel pretty much the same right now.

'So are you going to tell me why you're back here in my house?'

'It's not your house anymore and you don't deserve an explanation.'

'OK, I really don't care. You can have her. Maybe it'll be a good thing as it'll get her off my back.'

It's obvious that he really does care.

'Your son sounds upset. Shouldn't you go up and comfort him?'

'That's ironic, taking fatherhood advice from you.'

I know that he's referring to the problems I had with my low sperm count.

He smiles at me knowing that he's made his point and then leaves without saying another word to me, Karen or Sam.

Throughout our conversation the thumping on the wall in Sam's bedroom continued. I can faintly hear

Karen talking to Sam, presumably attempting to calm him down.

As I try to take in what just happened I help myself to another beer and wait another half an hour before Karen reappears.

'Danny, I'm so sorry about that. Sam texted Rob earlier and told him you were here. I didn't know he did that.'

'There's no need to apologise. How's Sam?'

'Still upset. The combination of Rob slamming the door and not being able to see his father when he knew he was downstairs has pushed him over the edge. It'll take another couple of hours before he fully calms down.'

'I should leave.'

'If you don't mind. I need to take care of Sam.'

'Of course.'

'Did Rob give you a hard time when I was upstairs?'

'Only a couple of gloating comments. Nothing I can't handle.'

'Please don't let it put you off coming around again,' she pleads.

'I won't, I promise.'

The wall thumping is getting louder.

'I better go,' Karen says as she gives me a quick kiss on my cheek.

'I'll let myself out.'

CHAPTER SIX

'How was your Christmas?' Maria asks as she hands me a cup of coffee.

'Surreal.'

'In what way?'

'My ex-wife, Karen messaged me on facebook on Christmas Day and I actually went to see her on Boxing Day.'

'That's unbelievable. I thought you didn't want anything to do with her?'

'She seemed very keen to see me. I thought that something was wrong, maybe she was ill.'

'And was she?'

'No, but she's divorced from Rob.'

'The guy that she had the affair with?'

'Yeah and I saw him yesterday.'

'You went there again?'

'Tell me about it. I really don't know what I've got myself into. It's all a bit scary.'

'Did you beat the shit out of him?'

'No but it wasn't exactly a friendly encounter. That's not all, they have a son called Sam and he's autistic.'

'Holy shit. Don't tell me you're thinking of getting back together with her again?'

'No, absolutely not.'

'Thank God for that. It sounds like a fucking mess. Did you meet Sam?'

'Yes I did. He's a very strange boy. That's sounds awful doesn't it?'

'I'm assuming you haven't met any autistic people before?'

'No, I really don't know too much about autism and I'm not good around children. I just don't know what to say to them, so you can imagine how nervous I was with Sam.'

'Danny, take my advice and stay well clear. Too much aggro.'

'You're absolutely right. I was having second thoughts about seeing Karen again but up to the point when Rob suddenly appeared it was going well. My intention was to hear what she had to say about what went wrong in the last year of our marriage but I never got around to having that discussion. We just chatted like old times, it was nice.'

'Sounds very amicable. Could be a good time to step away.'

'I think you're probably right. Anyway enough about my problems, how was your Christmas?'

'Sitting on the sofa in my PJs watching *Only Fools and Horses* repeats and *White Christmas* for the umpteenth time.'

'All rather sad,' I reply, tongue in cheek.

'OK, let's get back to work,' she smiles as we walk towards our desks.

'Just one more thing, I've been thinking about what you said on Friday about going out for a drink, are you still up for that?' I ask.

'Yes, of course. It wasn't just the drink talking. Let's arrange something this week but go somewhere a little bit more private. I'm not sure I'm up for another evening with this lot,' she says, pointing to our colleagues.

'I couldn't agree more.'

I walk back to my desk with a spring in my step, which is a first for a Monday morning.

CHAPTER SEVEN

Later that night Karen rings me.

'I just wanted to re-iterate what I said about Rob. Please ignore anything he has to say. He's an idiot, just trying to make trouble.'

'Have you heard from him since?'

'He sent me a couple of texts but I just deleted them.'

'You didn't read them?'

'No point. He would've just continued with the same old drivel about you.'

'He didn't lose his temper but I could tell he wasn't happy.'

'It's his male ego. He's quite happy to see me struggle on my own, not bothering to share any of the responsibility but if any guy comes anywhere near me he gets really pissed off, more so this time because it's you. Changing the subject, Sam and I are going into London on Sunday, nothing special just strolling around Piccadilly Circus and Leicester Square, maybe getting a bite to eat. Do you fancy joining us?'

'I don't know…'

'I'll hide Sam's mobile so he doesn't text his father. Unlike most eleven-year-olds he doesn't use it much and it'll give us a chance to have a good chat without Rob interrupting us. There's so much we need to discuss.'

'I know it's been a bit overwhelming for you lately so I'll totally understand if you don't want to come,' she adds, picking up on my hesitancy.

'No, it's OK. All I normally do on a Sunday is a bit of shopping and tidying around the house. I'll be delighted to spend some time with you and Sam.'

'That's great. Is it OK to meet at Brixton tube at ten? Or is that too early?'

'No, that's fine. I'll see you then.'

An hour later I'm surfing the net and after looking at my usual websites – BBC, Facebook and YouTube I google autism again but it's a minefield. What interested me was the information about autism diagnosis and the tell-tale signs: avoiding eye contact, not smiling when you smile at them, getting very upset if they do not like a certain taste, smell or sound, repetitive movements such as flapping their hands, flicking their fingers or rocking their body, liking a strict daily routine and getting very upset if it changes. Also, finding it hard to make friends or preferring to be on their own, not seeming to understand what others are thinking or feeling – for example they may not recognise phases like 'break a leg' and the list goes on.

I read another article that stated if you have one autistic child and you're married the likelihood of divorce is eighty per cent due to the stress levels it puts on parents. Was Sam the reason why Karen and Rob split up? If not it must have been a contributory factor.

So after agreeing with Maria only a few hours ago that the Karen/Sam/Rob situation is too toxic and that

I should stay clear of it, I'm now going to spend a day out in London with my ex-wife and her son. She mentioned that it'll give us time to talk and that was probably the reason why I agreed to go. We'll be spending the day together but will Sam monopolise Karen's attention? It won't be long before I find out.

CHAPTER EIGHT

'You've heard all about my sordid past but I don't know too much about yours,' I say to Maria.

We're in a pub in Leicester Square on a cold December evening. I've been looking forward to this ever since Maria suggested it on our office Christmas do. I don't often socialise with my other work colleagues. They're only interested in chatting about hard drives or firewalls and by the end of my working day that's the last thing I want to talk about.

'There's not too much to say really,' Maria replies.

'Are you in a relationship now, if you don't mind me asking?'

'Actually I've only just split up with someone. We'd been going out for nearly eighteen months.'

'I'm sorry to hear that, what happened?'

'He told me that he wanted to have sex with as many women as possible before settling down.'

'Wow, that must've hurt.'

'You could say that but to be honest I suspected that he was seeing other women in the last few months. He was more distant and just seemed to be out most nights of the week. A few weeks ago he told me he spent the evening in the pub with a few of his mates but a couple of them are facebook friends of mine and the following day they posted photos of their boozy night and my fella was nowhere to be seen. I did ask him about it but he just told me he didn't want to be in the photos. He must've thought I was a simpleton. I was on the verge of breaking up with him but he just beat me to it.'

'With all respect that guy must be an imbecile. He'll soon discover that the grass isn't greener.'

Maria smiles at me and takes a sip of her wine.

For me she ticks all the boxes – she's tall, slim, with long dark hair and dark brown eyes but more important than that she's a kind and considerate person. I always suspected she was but getting to know her better confirmed it.

'I hope that experience hasn't put you off. We're not all sex crazed bastards.'

'I won't bore you with the details of my other relationships that went pear-shaped but suffice to say I've yet to meet a guy who has remained faithful. I'm obviously an expert at picking arseholes. So in answer to your question – yes, it has put me off. I'm not interested in starting another relationship right now, it's all too raw.'

'I totally get that, but please don't lose faith.'

'Advice from someone whose hardly dated in over a decade?' She replies, smiling.

'I know, I know… but sometimes it's a lonely existence.'

'Well, let's get lonely together,' she replies, clicking my glass.

We have a couple more drinks before leaving the pub.

'Thanks for such a lovely evening. You've almost convinced me that there are some decent men out there.'

'Shall I take that as a compliment?'

'That was my intention. Anyway I better get that train. I'll see you tomorrow.'

She leans forward and gently kisses me on my cheek before dashing off. I didn't even have the chance to tell her that I also enjoyed myself. It's been several years since I've been out socially with a woman and I'd forgotten how nice it feels.

CHAPTER NINE

I haven't had too much time to reflect on my evening with Maria as the next morning I'm outside Brixton tube station waiting for Karen and Sam and feeling nervous. I always seem to agree to these meetings without actually thinking them through. All of a sudden my involvement with Karen has gone up another level and I feel uncomfortable about that. However, I have made my mind up that after today I won't see her again.

Although we haven't discussed much about how our marriage ended my conversations with Karen have been pleasant, which has surprised me, but it seems like a good moment to draw a line under it all as Maria suggested.

My life in the last ten years has been peaceful. I come and go as I please. I do miss being in a relationship sometimes, but I'm used to being on my own and that's the way I'd like my life to continue; for now anyway.

I hope to have a nice day with Karen and Sam and then I'll say my goodbyes but I've got to be strong and maybe that's why I'm feeling anxious.

A few minutes later I see Karen and Sam approaching and I notice a couple of guys walking past them look back at my ex-wife. She's wearing tight blue jeans, a red jumper and a black leather jacket. She looks like a model and I instantly think back to the day when I first met her.

It was nearly nineteen years ago. I had just finished university and was working part-time in a local pub when Karen came in with a group of her friends. They were all quite merry and played numerous dance records on the jukebox. Even though there was limited space in what was normally a quiet pub, the other women were up and dancing to every song. I noticed that Karen was the only one who didn't join in and when she went to the bar to order another round I asked her why. She told me that she had just split up from her boyfriend of two years and her friends had arranged this night out to cheer her up, but as they got increasingly inebriated they seemed to have forgotten the purpose of the evening.

I felt sorry for her and as my shift was about to finish I asked her if she wanted to go to another pub with me and she agreed. This was so out of character for me as I was a shy person who didn't have much success with women but there was something about her, apart from her good looks, that made me take that bold step.

By the end of the evening I politely kissed her cheek but didn't have the nerve to ask her out again, but as she was getting into the taxi she asked for my number, which I wrote on my tube ticket.

Rather than buy another ticket I walked home to Stockwell from Victoria trying to take in what an amazing and unexpected evening I had, but by the time I reached home I started to worry that she wouldn't call me and cursed myself for not getting her number.

I needn't have worried though as the next day she rang.

'A penny for your thoughts,' Karen says.

'Sorry, I was miles away. Thinking about what to get in Sainsbury's tomorrow.'

'You do lead an exciting life.'

'Hi ya, Sam, how are you today?' I ask.

'Your shoes look like a lump of shit. Can you polish them now?'

'It's OK, Sam, Danny will polish them when he gets home.'

'But he'll be walking around London with the shit shoes and everyone will be looking at us.'

'No they won't, don't worry about it.'

'Tesco have Kiwi Shine and Protect shoe polish, it's only two pounds and sixty pence. Quickly let's go there.'

'Sam, there's no need...' Karen implores.

'I don't want all those Piccadilly Circus Londoners shouting at us cos of his shoes.'

'It's no problem, let's go to Tesco's,' I say attempting to diffuse the situation.

'Sorry about that, Sam does have a thing about shoes...'

'It's fine.'

'Welcome to the autistic world.'

Tesco is only a few minutes' walk away. Sam guides me to the shoe polish section. I pay the lady two pounds and sixty pence and as I turn around Sam is standing right in front of me.

'You have to put the shoe polish on now.'

'Let's just do it outside,' Karen pleads with her son.

'No, the Tesco lady has to see that he's using the polish straight away otherwise she's going to be really pissed off.'

'It's OK,' I say as I step to one side, get down on one knee and polish both my shoes. Sam is kneeling alongside me and is pointing out parts I have missed.

'He's finished polishing both shoes Mrs Tesco,' Sam tells the bemused staff member.

Something tells me it's going to be a long day.

As we arrive on the tube station platform Sam delves into his back pack and pulls out what looks like ear plugs.

'He doesn't like the noise of the train,' Karen whispers to me.

When the train approaches Sam puts his hand over his ear plugs for extra protection. We get on the train and he leaves them on.

'Danny, I know this isn't the best time or place to have this conversation, but as Sam can't hear what we're saying I just want to chat about what happened to us.'

'What led you to it? Were things that bad between us?' I ask.

'No, not really but we were distant. You were away so much and I was lonely. Whenever I brought up your travelling you just dismissed it.'

'But it was all to make our life better.'

'I know but it wasn't easy for me. You've got to see that.'

'But why Rob?'

'Looking back on it now I can see that it was all pre-meditated on his behalf. He knew that you were away and came around a number of times before...'

Karen pauses, unable to say it.

'Did you encourage him?'

'Yes, I suppose I did. He was charming, attentive and I was flattered.'

'But you knew what he was like with women. Moving from one to the next without a second thought.'

'Yes I did, but at the time I was enjoying the company, someone to share my problems with.'

'And I'm sure he was a willing listener.'

'Yes he was.'

'Did you feel guilty at all? You must've known where it was leading?'

'Initially it was flirtation but then it got serious.'

'You didn't answer my question, did you feel guilty?'

'I know this sounds awful but the only time I felt remorseful was the night we... I really didn't think it would get to that point but from that moment I realised I had made a terrible mistake.'

'But you still continued to see him?'

She nods and looks down.

'Didn't you realise what an arsehole he was?'

'No, I didn't. It was only later when that became much clearer.'

'But you still married him?'

'Another mistake but it did give me Sam.'

The train pulls into Green Park station.

'We'll get off here and walk down to Piccadilly Circus,' Karen tells me.

Sam still has his ear plugs on as we go up the escalator. There's an awkward silence between myself and Karen. Although I'm pleased to have had this conversation, I didn't expect it to happen between Brixton and Green Park tube stations.

'Sorry. I know the subject deserves a lot more time but needs must,' Karen says, looking at her son.

'No need to apologise, I'm glad we spoke about it.'

'Why are you here anyway?' Sam suddenly asks me as he takes out his ear plugs.

'Sam, don't be so rude,' Karen says.

'But he's a stranger who doesn't like butter.'

'Your mum asked me to come along and I thought it'd be nice to get to know you a bit better,' I reply.

'Mum always told me to stay away from strangers.'

'Danny's not a stranger. Remember I told you that we were married a long time ago.'

'Does that mean you've seen him in his underpants?'

Karen blushes slightly and smiles at me, then nods at Sam.

'Did he wear socks with his underpants?'

'Sam, can we please stop talking about Danny's underpants. Now, where do you want to go?'

'There's too much noise, can we go where there aren't any cars?'

'That's a bit difficult in Central London.'

'What about going for a walk in Green Park?' I suggest.

'Do they have squirrels? I don't like them, they eat too fast. I can't eat food too fast cos it makes me go for a crap.'

'Sam, what have I told you about rude words?'

'But squirrels are always in a rush. They need to chill out. I think they're evil bastards.'

'Shall we take the risk?' I ask Karen who rolls her eyes at Sam's latest observation.

'Yeah why not? Who dares wins.'

Sam walks slightly ahead of us as we enter the park. He's constantly twisting his head left to right as if he's watching a tennis match. Presumably he's looking out for any evil bastards.

'I really thought that you would've remarried,' Karen tells me.

'I haven't dated anyone for quite a while.'

'Why's that?'

'To be honest, I was so hurt after our split that I couldn't face the risk of going through that again.'

'Oh, Danny, I'm so sorry…'

'No, don't be sorry, it's something I need to change. I can't go on living my life being negative about relationships.'

'I was so wrapped up with having Sam and all the problems that came with that I didn't reach out to you as much as I should've, but my guilt never left me.'

'You've had enough to deal with since we were last together so please don't give it a moment's thought. You've done an amazing job bringing up Sam without much help from Rob. I really don't know how you've coped.'

I notice that Sam has stopped his tennis match-style head movements and is walking back to us.

'Are you going to be following us all day?' Sam asks me.

'Well yes, I'll be spending the day with you and your mum.'

'What are your hobbies?' Sam inquires.

'I don't really have any. Apart from collecting ants do you have any more?' I ask.

'Eating.'

Does that classify as a hobby I wonder?

'What's your favourite food?' I inquire.

'Number ten is warm Coca-Cola, number nine is salt and vinegar crisps, number eight is oranges without the pips, number seven is Twirls, number six is salami, number five is doughnuts, number four is shepherd's pie, number three is steak and kidney pie, number two is toast, but only on white bread, and number one is Rice Krispies. I love the noise Rice Krispies makes when I pour the milk onto them, it's always the best moment of my day.'

'That's nice,' is all I manage to say.

'Anyway, Mum all this grass is making me sweat can we go back onto the pavement now?'

We walk around for a while and end up in the Hard Rock Café at Hyde Park Corner. The waitress approaches us.

'Hi, my name's Sandy and I'll be your waitress for today. Are you ready to order?'

'And my name is Sam and I like playing with ants.'

'And what would you like to eat, Sam?' The waitress nonchalantly replies as if she has heard the ants anecdote several times during the course of her working day.

'I like burgers but not with all that lettuce and tomato crap in the middle.'

'OK, a plain burger it is. Now how would you like it done?'

'He'll have it well done and with fries please,' Karen says.

'Fries are my thirteenth favourite food,' Sam adds.

I can feel a top twenty coming on.

'Salad?'

'No way, humans shouldn't be eating that shit. Just give it to rabbits and hamsters – they don't know what they're eating cos they're stupid.'

Shortly afterwards Karen and I order our meal.

'Do you like rain?' Sam asks me.

'What do you mean?'

'You know rain. It comes from the sky. You've seen it before.'

'I prefer the sun.'

'But the sun makes my eyes squint and I have to take off my jumper. I like wearing jumpers.'

'That's good to hear.'

I look at Karen in the hope she will intervene but she's looking at her mobile. This type of conversation must be normal to her but I'm struggling right now.

'Rain is much better. It tickles my nose and makes me want to laugh. Anyway what do you think of James Bond?'

'I like the Bond films.'

'Who's your favourite James Bond?'

'Roger Moore.'

'But Roger Moore died on the twenty-third of May two thousand and seventeen. He was eighty-nine years old. He should've stayed alive until his ninetieth birthday on October the fourteenth and he would've had a fantastic birthday party. Maybe he just didn't like parties?'

There's no answer to that.

'You can't have a favourite James Bond if they're dead. It has to be between Daniel Craig, who is fifty-four, Pierce Brosnan, who is sixty-nine, George Lazenby, who is eight-three or Timothy Dalton, who is seventy-six.'

'OK, fair enough. Out of that lot I would pick Daniel Craig.'

'But he always looked pissed off. Doesn't he like being James Bond?'

'OK, Sam, I think we've exhausted the James Bond conversation now,' Karen adds.

'Who is your favourite?' I ask.

'I haven't got one.'

When Sam's burger arrives he puts tomato ketchup on the top, in the middle and even the bottom of the bun. He does the same with the malt vinegar.

The rest of the meal passes without Sam saying too much more. I'm enjoying catching up with Karen and feeling increasingly guilty about what I have to do later.

As we're heading towards the tube station Sam rushes over and licks the post box (as you do).

'Sam, stop licking the post box, it's dirty,' Karen tells her son.

'It's delicious, but not as tasty as the one on our road. Anyway it's not a post box it's a mailbox. The Americans say mailbox and they really know what they're talking about.'

'Why does he do that?' I quietly ask Karen.

'Autistic children and adults have a lot of sensory issues which usually means they are either over sensitive or under sensitive to sight, sounds, smell, taste, touch and so on. Sam cannot pass a post... mailbox without giving it a good lick.'

'Does anyone ever say anything to you when he's doing this?'

'Not really but a lot of people just stop and stare, which I sort of understand but then anyone with half a brain should realise that something was not quite right. Maybe I'm just being over sensitive. Sometimes I tell them to take a photo, it'll last longer. They move on after that.'

'I know very little about autism.'

'I knew nothing until Sam was diagnosed.'

'Mum, there's an American sweet shop over there, I want to get some Hershey's chocolate,' Sam excitedly says, pointing to a shop on the other side of the street.

'OK then,' she replies.

'Does he like everything American?' I ask.

'Tell me about it. He's on to me nearly every day about going there. Hopefully one day we will.'

In his eagerness to get to the sweet shop Sam dashes into the road oblivious to the traffic but Karen quickly grabs him back and pushes him onto the pavement just before a speeding car hits her as she attempts to follow him back. The impact lifts her into the air and she lands on the bonnet with her face against the windscreen. I can see that her eyes are closed. The car carries on a few yards before stopping. The driver stares at Karen but rather than getting out of the car decides to restart it as Karen falls heavily to the ground hitting her head on the road. It all happened too fast for me to intervene.

The car speeds away.

I rush over to her.

'Karen can you hear me?'

She doesn't move.

CHAPTER TEN

The ambulance arrives ten minutes later. Karen has been motionless since her fall.

'Can you tell me exactly what happened?' One of the two paramedics asks me.

'Her son ran into the road. She managed to grab him but a car hit her. She hasn't moved since.'

'Was the car traveling at speed?'

'Well over the speed limit I'd say.'

'Can you tell me what part of her body had the biggest impact?'

'Her hip maybe? She actually landed on the car bonnet but she looked unconscious even then. Her head hit the ground when she fell.'

'What's her name?'

'Karen.'

'Karen, can you hear me?' The paramedic asks.

There's no response.

They check her pulse and put her in a recovery position. I recognise this as I took a First Aid course last year. I feel guilty that I didn't do this myself but I had been watching Sam.

The police arrive and cordon off the area.

Sam is staring blankly at his mother. What's going through his mind right now I wonder?

'Don't worry, Sam, your mum will be OK,' I say more confidently than I feel.

'Is she dead?' He asks as if he didn't hear me.

'No, but she'll have to go to hospital.'

'How is she going to get on the tube?'

'The ambulance will take her and they'll be able to go through all the red lights to get her there as quickly as possible.'

'But the policemen will arrest her.'

'No, they won't. The ambulance has special permission to go through red lights.'

'I don't want my mother going to jail.'

'That won't happen so don't worry.'

'Will she still be able to take me to Comic Con in May?'

'Yes, I'm sure she will.'

'Excuse me, sir, sorry to bother you at this time but can you tell me exactly what happened?' A policeman asks.

'Can we discuss this at the hospital? I need to be with my ...' I reply.

'I understand, sir. An officer will drive you there as soon as the ambulance leaves.'

Karen is now on a stretcher and gently being manoeuvred into the ambulance.

A policeman invites Sam and me into the back of his car and we follow the ambulance. Sam looks out at the busy London streets.

'Excuse me policeman, what's your name?'

'Robert.'

'Policeman Robert, is my mum going to make me toast tomorrow morning?'

'I think maybe your father will have to do that,' he replies, looking at me.

'I'm not his father,' I reply.

Suddenly a tinny voice comes through on the policeman's radio but I can't make out what's being said. As soon as the message ends the policeman turns to look at Sam.

'Your mother is talking and asking where you are.'

'I'm here of course.'

'It appears to be a hip injury and it may even be broken but we'll find out soon enough,' the policeman says to us both.

CHAPTER ELEVEN

Sam and I have been sitting in the hospital's A&E department for just over two hours.

I don't know what to say to him as I haven't got a clue what the latest news of Karen is. It was encouraging that she came round in the ambulance but we haven't had any update since.

Sam hasn't spoken much apart from asking the man sitting next to him whether he wore pyjamas in bed or just his underpants and vest. The man looked confused (I sympathise) but when I explained Sam's autism he relaxed and replied that his favourite pyjamas were sky blue in colour and then asked Sam if he wore pyjamas. Sam ignored the question and continued to read his book and soon afterwards a man in a white coat approaches us.

'Hello, it's Danny, isn't it?'

I nod.

'I've been examining your wife and I can confirm that she has a broken hip and will require surgery. It's scheduled for tomorrow morning.'

'Is she going to be OK?' I ask.

'Yes, it's a fairly straight forward procedure. I'm very confident that she'll be able to make a full recovery.'

'What exactly does the surgery involve?'

'We'll be inserting metal screws into her hip bone to hold it together while the fracture heals. I don't foresee any problems.'

'How long will she be in hospital?'

'Three days, maybe a bit more. A physical therapist will visit her to go through rehabilitation exercises a couple of times a week. Someone will have to stay with her for a while as she'll be quite fragile and will need a lot of care but we can discuss this more tomorrow. It's important that she gets a good night's rest in preparation for the surgery.'

'Is it possible to see her?'

'Yes, but only for a few minutes. We're given her some strong pain killers which will make her drowsy.'

While he was speaking Sam has been reading a book about Post Offices. I'm told that it's a fascinating read.

'Sam, shall we go and see your mother?'

'Yeah, OK. I want to tell her about my Post Office facts.'

'Why don't you tell me first?'

'There are eleven thousand, six hundred and thirty-eight Post Offices in the United kingdom. I've been to four but I'd love to visit all of them.'

Aren't they all the same?

'They sell lots of different coloured stamps. The first class stamp is both red and purple and the second class stamp is blue and green. Whenever Mum buys a book of first class stamps I never know what colour the stamps are going to be, it confuses me. The stamp to America is...'

'OK, we better go and see your mum now cos she's going to sleep soon,' I interrupt.

'So you hate stamps then?'

'No, I really don't mind them. Let's talk about this after we've seen your mum, OK?'

'Oh, alright,' Sam replies, sounding disappointed.

I find it strange that he seems more interested in Post Offices than his mothers' health but maybe that's just a coping mechanism? What the hell do I know?

As we're walking down the corridor with the doctor Sam stops, opens one of the doors and peeps in.

'Are all the people in these rooms dead?' He asks the doctor.

'No, most of them will need operations but in time they'll be OK.'

'But you must have some dead people in this building. Can I see them?'

The doctor looks at me with a concerned expression.

'Do you throw them out of the window when they've popped their clogs?'

'He's autistic,' I say.

He smiles at us both. 'No, all the patients are fighting fit.'

'So nobody dies in this hospital?' Sam inquires.

'Here's your mother's room,' the doctor replies, avoiding the question.

Karen looks up and smiles weakly at us as we enter the room. Various tubes are attached to her, all linked to monitoring machines. It's a sad sight.

Sam rushes to her but a nurse gently intercepts him.

'Will you be able to take me to Comic Con on Saturday the thirteenth of May?' He asks.

She nods and holds out her hand which he takes.

'What about making breakfast tomorrow?'

'I'm afraid not, I'll still be in here.'

'You can let her go home now, she's talking fine,' Sam tells the doctor.

'No, I'm sorry, your mum needs an operation in the morning.'

'But can't you do that at home after breakfast?'

'It has to be in the hospital, but don't worry she'll be home soon enough.'

'Nurse, would you mind taking Sam outside for a few minutes? I just want to have a private chat with Danny. It won't take long.'

The nurse smiles at Sam and together they leave the room. The doctor follows them both.

'Are you in a lot of pain?' I ask.

'They injected me with something when I first arrived and that helped but if I make any movement it kills me.'

'I'm so sorry, Karen, if I hadn't distracted you none of this would've happened.'

'That's bullshit. All we were doing was talking. It's totally my fault. Sam runs into the road frequently, I should've been holding his hand. He's totally my responsibility and my negligence almost killed him.'

'But you saved his life.'

A tear trickles down her face as she shakes her head.

'Please don't get too upset. Things may look bleak right now but Sam's doing OK and the doctor says you'll make a full recovery. Do you want me to contact Rob?'

'No, not yet.'

'But surely he has to look after Sam?'

'There's no way my son will be moving in with him even on a temporary basis. That's never going to happen.'

'Perhaps this isn't the best time to be discussing this. I can see that you're distressed. I'll take Sam to wherever you want me to.'

The doctor pops his head in.

'Excuse me, Danny we really have to medicate Karen now, so I'm afraid you'll have to leave.'

'Just a few more minutes please,' Karen says and he leaves.

'My parents are too old to be looking after Sam and Belinda's off to America tomorrow.'

'OK, so who does that leave?'

She looks at me for what seems like an eternity before replying.

'You.'

'But I've no idea how to look after an autistic boy. There must be someone else?'

'I realise I'm asking a massive favour but I have complete trust in you. If you could just stay with Sam in my house tonight we can work things out tomorrow after the operation.'

'But who's going to suddenly care for him between now and then that you haven't thought of?'

'Excuse me, Danny, I really have to ask you to leave now,' the doctor says upon entering the room.

When I look at Karen I see a woman in great pain and frightened at the prospect of an operation. How can I refuse?

'It's OK, Karen, I'll look after Sam. Are your house keys in your handbag?' I ask.

She smiles and nods. I take the keys, wish her good luck and leave her with the doctor.

I lean on the wall outside the room and can see Sam in the waiting room with the nurse. He's still reading his Post Office book. What the hell have I got myself into? My mind drifts back to Karen's Christmas Day Facebook message. The message led me to believe that something was wrong so how could I not answer it? But I never thought that replying would lead to this? At the start of today I had made my mind up not to get involved in Karen and Sam's life but now I feel like I'm in over my head.

I walk into the waiting room. The nurse smiles and leaves.

'Hi, Sam. Your mum asked me to take you home.'

'Is she just pretending to be ill cos she wants to get a good nights' kip? She's always saying that I keep her up at night but I don't like sleeping. I think that sleeping is a silly thing to do.'

'No she was hurt badly. You heard the doctor say that she needs an operation.'

'I don't like him. He has too many wrinkles on his face.'

'Shall we go?'

He reluctantly follows me to the exit. I find it very odd that he hasn't grasped the seriousness of the situation. After all he was right next to her when the car hit Karen so hard.

As we're about to leave the policeman who drove us to the hospital approaches us. I had told him what I knew while waiting earlier.

'Thanks for all your information. We managed to identify the vehicle through one of the roadside CCTV cameras and the driver is in police custody right now.'

'Well I hope they throw the book at that bastard. What sort of a bloke knocks over a pedestrian and leaves her for dead?'

'It happens all too often I'm afraid, but rest assured he's going to be in a lot of trouble. Anyway, thanks again, and I hope your partner gets better soon,' he says and walks away.

Throughout the journey 'home' Sam is quiet. Is he thinking about his mother or what Post Office is next on his list to visit?

Given what Karen said about Sam's tendency to rush into oncoming traffic I am virtually glued to him the whole time. I would feel better if I could hold his hand but I'm afraid that he might freak out if I did. I'm keen to get him into his house as soon as possible. We only stop twice for Sam to lick two post... sorry, mailboxes.

It's a strange feeling entering the house with only Sam alongside of me.

'Do you want anything to eat?' I ask Sam.

'I'll wait till Mum's back. I don't want you poisoning me,' he says before dashing upstairs. We did have dinner a few hours ago so I'm assuming he's not hungry.

I am surprised that Karen was so against Sam staying with his father. Is there a dark history that I'm not aware of? I remember her saying that she hid Sam's phone so he wouldn't contact his father. I really don't want to deal with Rob right now.

I look in the fridge and see there's a few cans of beer so I help myself to one. Without sounding like an alcoholic I need a drink more than ever right now. As I settle down on the sofa I start to think of the practicalities of the situation I'm in. I have an important work meeting first thing tomorrow morning – how can I possibly attend that? I'm working on another project with extremely tight deadlines and this meeting was going to clarify some of the issues that I have. Peter, my boss, is very demanding so I suspect he's not going to be too understanding with my current predicament.

Work is everything to him, a personal life is not important as far as he's concerned. I'm really not looking forward to having that conversation.

Then there's Sam's school. I presume he has to attend tomorrow? I've no idea what school he goes to so I'm relying on Sam to help me out on this one.

Karen gave me absolutely no guidelines on how to deal with Sam but I can't really blame her for that in the circumstances. But I still can't get over the fact that I'm the only person in her life who can take care of her son. I totally understand why she's reluctant to hand Sam over to her parents but I'm still baffled about why she's so anti-Rob. Surely she must have other friends or relatives that can step in? I decide to check in on Sam and tentatively knock on his bedroom door.

'Sam, can I come in?'

'No.'

'Why not?'

'Because you haven't had a bath. I don't want any germs in my room.'

'If I have a bath can I come in?'

'No, I don't trust Vauxhall people.'

'How are you feeling?'

'Like dog turd.'

'Please don't worry too much, we should find out tomorrow when your mum's coming home.'

'Why did that Piccadilly Circus driver want to kill my mother? Didn't he like the clothes she was wearing?'

'He didn't try to kill her, it's just he was driving too fast and your mum was still on the road after pulling you back.'

'But I wanted to get some Hershey's chocolate. I asked the policeman if I could get some before we went to that hospital but he didn't want to. So the driver was a bastard and so was that policeman.'

'I promise you, Sam, I'll order some Hershey's chocolate for you online. Would that make you feel a bit better?'

'Will the chocolate taste if it's ordered online? I like chocolate bought in a shop.'

'No, it's exactly the same. Anyway, I need to take you to school tomorrow. Do you walk to school?'

'Yes, it's seven hundred and fifty-two steps and takes eleven minutes when I do it with Mum but it's probably going to be slower if you have to come with me.'

'What time do you start?'

'Nine o'clock but I always get there at eight-fifty-one which means that I have to leave the house at eight-forty. Do you know how to make Rice Krispies? If not just look it up on YouTube.'

'That's not a problem, I'll do that for you. You get a good nights' sleep and I'll wake you up so you can get ready for school.'

'No need to do that. I get up at three fifty-five every morning. I don't want to be late for school cos it'll give me a headache all day.'

I always thought that parents struggled to get their kids ready for school on time – obviously not in this household.

'OK sleep well.'

'And don't forget about the Hershey's chocolate.'

I would guess that if the parent of a 'normal' eleven-year-old child was involved in a serious car accident the child would probably be extremely upset and tearful. Sam on the other hand seems more pissed off that he couldn't get his chocolate while his mother lays in a hospital bed awaiting an operation for a broken hip.

DENIS DEASY

I need to speak to Maria, so I ring her.

'Maria, I'm sorry to disturb you on a Sunday night but I've got a big problem.'

'What's the matter?'

'I went into London with Karen and Sam…'

'Hold on, I thought that you were going knock that on the head?'

'Yes, that was my intention but things have changed. I was going to end it after our trip but she got hit by a car and is in hospital.'

'Oh my God, is she OK?'

'She's got a broken hip and is being operated on tomorrow but that's not all. I'm staying overnight with Sam and I haven't a clue how to look after him. He makes me so nervous.'

'So what's your way out of this?'

'I don't know right now. Karen's accident has really complicated things.'

'Without wishing to sound cold hearted it's not your problem. Where's her ex in all of this?'

'She doesn't want him involved.'

'Danny, it's a mess. I don't understand what any of this has got to do with you. Was she drugged up after the accident and not thinking clearly?'

'She seemed a bit out of it but after what happened that's understandable. I do feel partly responsible for the accident.'

'Why's that?'

'Sam ran into the road to get to a sweet shop on the other side but Karen managed to pull him back onto the pavement. However she was hit by a speeding car. I was talking to her at the moment Sam decided to go on his suicide mission. She was distracted.'

'You can't blame yourself for that.'

'That's what Karen said but just before it happened we were talking about our past and I can't help thinking I distracted her from watching Sam.'

'Danny, I've never met Karen and I do feel sorry for her and her boy but an elderly uncle of mine broke his hip last year and he fully recovered from it so without knowing the full extent of Karen's injury I'd say that there's a good chance that she'll recover too.'

'Yeah, the doctor thinks so.'

'OK, you have to look after Sam tonight and for some time tomorrow which isn't ideal but it's only a few hours and then someone else will take over so don't panic.'

'But I'm worried it's not as simple as that. What if she can't get anyone else?'

'I'm pretty sure she will. Everything will look a lot clearer tomorrow. Are you still OK for the eight-thirty meeting?'

'I can't make it. I have to take Sam to school so I'll speak to Peter in a minute.'

'He's going to do his nut. It took him ages to arrange this meeting with all the suppliers.'

'I feel awful but what can I do? I know he's an arrogant prick but surely he'll understand, given the circumstances?'

'Do you remember when we were working until ten o'clock on Christmas Eve a couple of years ago?'

'Yeah, point taken. Sorry again for disturbing you. I'll text you after I talk to Peter.'

'No problem, just take it easy and make sure you get yourself out of this situation as soon as possible.'

Without further ado I ring Peter.

'Hello, Danny, what's up?' He's not one for small talk.

'I'm afraid I won't be able to make the meeting tomorrow.'

'You're kidding me.'

'No, my ex-wife was in a car accident today and I have to look after her autistic son.'

'He's not your son then?'

'No.'

'Where's the father?'

'She doesn't want anything to do with him.'

'Danny, you have to make this meeting. They're all coming over from Chicago, straight from the airport to the meeting. There's a lot of pressure to get this in on time.'

'Maria can handle all their questions. I can liaise with her afterwards.'

'They're expecting to see you, Danny, this is non-negotiable.'

'Peter, I understand the importance of the meeting but I have to take Sam to school at the same time as the meeting. It's impossible for me to get there. I'm sorry.'

'Your contract's up for renewal soon isn't it?'

'Yes, in two weeks.'

'Well I won't be renewing it so you're now off the project. Maria's going to take the lead on this. Whenever you can find the time please pop into the office and collect your stuff. Good luck with your school run.'

I'm totally shocked. Not for a second did I think I would lose my job over this. I work as an IT consultant for *FixIT* which means I'm not a permanent employee. I have worked there for five years. My contract is for six months and for the past five years they have always renewed me. I get paid more than the permanent staff and one of the reasons for this is I can hit the ground running on their IT projects as I'm qualified in many IT programming languages. However this couldn't have happened at a worse time as I'm in the process of building a loft extension which is costing me forty grand. I need to get another job as soon as possible but the prospect of going through the interview process again after such a long time fills me with dread.

The drawback with being an IT consultant is that your contract can be terminated at any time and with no notice. Consultants are not protected in the same way that permanent employees are and some managers take advantage of this. In my IT career I've seen many abrupt termination of contracts but never one due to non-attendance at a meeting, no matter how important that meeting may have been.

The project that I was due to manage was going to bring in a lot of revenue to *FixIT* so to some extent I can understand Peter's frustration but I really think he over reacted. Maria won't be too thrilled with the extra responsibility and pressure. I decide against texting her. She'll find out soon enough, if not already.

I never liked working for Peter. He is egotistical and self-centred. He didn't once ask if Karen was OK. I'm afraid lager won't do it for me tonight, it has to be something stronger. I find a bottle of brandy in the kitchen cabinet and pour myself a glass. By the time I'm on my second I reflect on my current situation and come to the conclusion that like Peter I am also self-centred. It comes from living on my own for so many years. My mother used to say that there's always someone worse off and that I don't have to look too far to find that person. My ex-wife is in hospital right now with a broken hip while her autistic son is telling her to get out of bed to make his breakfast.

Yes, there's always someone worse off but that doesn't make me feel any better right now so I take another sip of brandy while I ponder my situation.

CHAPTER TWELVE

I wake up with a slight hangover and the realisation that I am now jobless.

Peter has done this in the past but has changed his mind so my hope is that he will do the same for me or am I deluding myself?

The bed that I slept in last night was the same one that I once shared with Karen all those years ago and brought back some fond memories. Those happy reminiscences soon evaporate when I think about what her and Rob got up to in it.

I go downstairs to find Sam sitting on the sofa watching *Popeye*.

'You like *Popeye* then?'

'Yeah, his pipe is amazing.'

'Have you had breakfast?'

'No, I'll wait for Mum to come back.'

'She's having her operation this morning so she can't make it for you today. Will you let me do it?'

'I don't trust margarine people. You'll put that weak, shitty milk on my Rice Krispies.'

'I'll use the full milk; you can watch me.'

'No, it's better I starve.'

He's obviously very wary of me and I understand that. When I drop him off at school I'll have a word with his teacher about his reluctance to eat.

'I have to leave in twelve minutes so can you have a bath now? I don't want everyone at school to smell your stinky feet cos they're gross and don't wear the same underpants too, that'll make me vomit onto the pavement. You can wear my mum's knickers.'

I don't think my feet reek but Karen told me that he's extremely sensitive to smells and I'm definitely not going down the cross dressing route just yet. Two licked mailboxes later we arrive at the school entrance.

'Hello, Sam, where's your mum?' A female teacher asks.

'She's in hospital, so this stranger brought me,' he replies, pointing at me.

'Oh my God, what happened?'

'She couldn't come home to make my breakfast this morning so I'm starving.'

'Hello, my name's Danny. I'm Karen's ex-husband. She had a road accident yesterday afternoon and broke her hip. She's having an operation this morning and that's why I'm here. She's expected to make a full recovery but for the next few weeks someone else will be dropping Sam off. Once we know who that will be I'm sure Karen will let you know.' I am quick to rule myself out of contention.

'He's an alien to me but my mum has seen him in his underpants,' Sam chips in.

'I'm glad she's recovering but normally we need official notification if someone other than Karen drops Sam off. Can I see some identification please?' The teacher asks.

'I'm afraid I've left my wallet at Sam's house. Obviously Karen wasn't able to let you know. I'm sure you understand.'

'And he's wearing my mum's knickers,' Sam adds.

'Rest assured I'm not. In the interests of clarity I'm wearing Karen's most recent ex's underpants,' I tell the increasingly suspicious teacher.

'Let me explain,' I add, 'I stayed with Sam last night and as I didn't have a chance to go home I am wearing Rob's old clothes. Presumably you know Rob?'

'Yes, I do, but where is he? Surely he should be looking after his son?'

'Karen didn't want him to know about the accident,' I quietly tell her.

She looks questioningly at me.

'I know. Please take it up with Karen when you see her.'

After chatting a little longer with the teacher I manage to convince her that I'm not a child abductor or a cross-dresser. I give her my contact details and head back to Vauxhall. Within seconds of arriving home I am naked. I detested wearing that bastard's clothes.

Later that morning I contact the hospital to learn that Karen's operation is a success but she won't be released from the hospital for at least a couple of days. I will visit her after I pick Sam up from school.

My life has been turned upside down in the last forty-eight hours as I was on the verge of letting Karen know that it's time to go our separate ways. To be honest I was getting increasingly nervous about telling her face-to-face so I was thinking of letting her know via a private Facebook message later. I realise that this is a cowards' way out but hopefully she would have understood.

Our short reunion has perhaps healed guilt feelings for us both. However, now it's more complicated. I can't afford the time to look after Sam or Karen. I need to get my CV updated and contact employment agencies as a matter of urgency.

I still can't believe Peter terminated my contract in such circumstances. Will he change his mind? I'm hoping Maria will be able to clarify the situation so I ring her.

'Hi, Maria, how did it go today?'

'I think it's safe to say that it isn't only Peter who's pissed off with you. All of the clients are fucked off cos it means there's going to be a delay.'

'Then why doesn't he just let me come back?'

'There's no way Peter's going to change his mind, he made that quite clear today even if it means prolonging the deadlines. You know what's he's like.'

'I'm really sorry for landing you in it.'

'I know what happened yesterday was a freak accident but I told you to cut ties with her. I don't understand why you needed to see her again?'

'Neither do I. I've lost my job because of that decision.'

'And I'm going to be working day and night for the next six weeks because of it.'

'I can't apologise enough.'

'Don't worry, I'll get through it.'

The flirting and fun night we had a couple of days ago seems very distant now.

We talk a little more before saying our goodbyes. I can tell that she already feels under great pressure and I know it's my fault. But she's too nice to have a go at me. I just wish I could help her.

Any faint hope I had of getting my job back has been extinguished.

CHAPTER THIRTEEN

By mid-afternoon I make my way back to Sam's school.

'Not you again,' an exasperated Sam shouts as I approach the front entrance. Not the best greeting I've had recently.

'That's not nice, Sam. Danny's been very kind to look after you while your mum's in hospital,' a teacher tells him.

'But he's crap,' Sam quickly replies.

I am hoping that Karen will tell me that my guardian duties are over when we see her shortly. If anyone is feeling aggrieved it should be me – looking after Sam has cost me my job.

'Will you be dropping him off again tomorrow morning?' The teacher asks.

'I don't know. I'll call the school after I see Karen.'

Sam doesn't utter a word during the car journey and I'm also at a loss to know what to say.

'So what's your favourite subject?' I finally ask.

'I like going for a wee at lunchtime. It's quiet in the toilet. I go into the cubicle. Nobody speaks to me in there.'

'Don't you like people talking to you?'

'Only when my ears are in a listening mood.'

Sam's not alone there.

'Are your ears in a listening mood now?'

'No.'

I pick up on his subtle hint and don't try to engage him in conversation as we make our way to the hospital.

Karen smiles as we enter her room.

'How's my boy?' She asks, her voice barely a whisper.

'You must've finished your medicine by now? Can you just get your clothes on and come home to cook me some chips and a steak and kidney pie?'

'Sam, my hip's really painful. I'm going to stay in hospital tonight and maybe tomorrow night as well.'

'Has the medicine made you lazy?'

She smiles and holds Sam's hand.

A nurse enters the room.

'The doctor will be here in a few minutes. He needs to examine Karen so I'm afraid you'll have to leave while he's doing this,' she says to me.

'Can I ask you a big favour? Would you mind taking my son to the vending machine?' Karen asks. 'I want to have a quick word with Danny.' She reaches for her handbag but I hand the nurse some coins.

'Of course, I understand.'

'Can I get Skittles?' Sam asks his mother.

Karen nods.

'That's amazing. You never let me have Skittles. That medicine must be amazing.'

'So how are you feeling?' I ask, as Sam and the nurse leave the room.

'Relieved that the operation went OK but I'm in a lot of pain. It's going to take a while before I can do things I took for granted yesterday.'

'I hate to pressurise you, Karen but who's going to look after Sam now? I have to let the school know.'

'If you could take care of Sam tonight I would be so grateful. I haven't had a chance to sort anything and I can't think of anyone right now.'

'Oh, come on, Karen. I can't be your only option.'

'When I got with Rob I lost contact with most of my friends. I still see Kathy, Emily and Alice but they're all single and I wouldn't trust them to look after Sam.'

'Have you forgotten that I'm also single?'

'But you've always been very responsible.'

'OK but you have to let Rob know. He'll go ballistic when he finds out I've been looking after his son.'

'I can't…'

'Why?'

'He's totally incapable of looking after Sam. It's as simple as that.'

'Are you going to tell him about your accident?'

'When I'm physically and mentally better. He doesn't see Sam from one month to the next so he'll be oblivious to all of this.'

'Is there something you're not telling me about Rob?'

'Apart from the fact that he's a selfish prick? But you know that already.'

'I know that your parents are getting on a bit but can't they look after Sam for a while?'

'No, they'll be too freaked out and won't be able to stop him running into the road.'

'Of course, I didn't think about that. What about contacting Social Services to get some respite care? They must've dealt with these type of emergencies before.'

'The very few times I've had respite care it's been a total disaster. When I picked Sam up from the respite centre all I got was a series of complaints. Sometimes they would call me to collect him early and the really annoying thing is Sam didn't do much wrong. He's special needs so he's never going to act normal. They were giving me a hard time because of his autism. I expect that from people who are not clued up on autism but staff members are supposed to be trained to deal with autistic type behaviours. Maybe I was unlucky and got the wrong care workers to look after him but I was so pissed off with the way he was treated I didn't bother with it in the end.'

'I'm sorry to hear that.'

'How are you getting on with him?' She asks.

'To be honest, I'm finding it really difficult. I don't know what to say to him and it's quite clear he doesn't like me.'

'He can't handle any change of routine, it makes him anxious but you'll win him over.'

'He said I was crap when I picked him up from school.'

Karen giggles and winces in pain as she caresses her hip.

'Sorry, I promise I won't make you laugh again.'

Karen smiles at me. She's obviously struggling and I can't help but feel protective towards her. Mostly I want to run away from all this and then I feel guilty complaining to her about looking after her autistic son.

'I'm sorry to drag you into this, Danny. I just don't know who else to turn to right now. Maybe I should try to get in contact with Social Services again but I'm not sure they would be agreeable to staying at my house for any length of time. I certainly don't want Sam going anywhere else; that would freak him out.'

'Don't worry, Karen. I'll stay with him tonight and we'll talk again tomorrow. Just get some rest.'

'Thanks, Danny. I don't deserve your kindness.'

Shortly afterwards the doctor enters the room so I say my goodbyes and meet up with Sam in the corridor.

'So she can't be bothered getting out of bed again?' Sam tells me after I explain to him about Karen staying at the hospital.

'Your mother has broken her hip and needs to stay here for a while to get better. She's in a lot of pain right now.'

'I still think she's faking it. Why doesn't she just take one of those paracetamol tablets? That'll cure her hip.'

'Paracetamol tablets are not strong enough.'

'Just tell her to take loads of them. It'll be fine.'

I hope his future careers teacher doesn't suggest that Sam goes into the medical profession.

'Anyway, I want my dad to look after me. He lives somewhere in Streatham. If we drive through Streatham and shout his name he'll come out to get me.'

'Your father's busy right now so tonight I'll be looking after you again.'

'Shit on it.'

I have to refrain from laughing at his comment. Karen did tell me yesterday that he's beginning to swear more recently which is obviously a concern for her.

'How about going out for a meal?' I suggest.

'OK, I want to go to Gordon Simmonds restaurant in Chelsea. It's called Gordon's.'

The combination of Gordon Simmonds and Chelsea sounds very expensive to me.

'How about going to Wetherspoons in Brixton instead?'

'Last year when I was coming back from watching those Chelsea footballers kicking a ball on grass I asked

Dad if we could go to Gordon's and he told me to get lost so we went to McDonalds instead.'

Is Sam clever enough to blackmail me into going to this damn restaurant?

'I take it you like Gordon Simmonds?' I ask.

'I like the white jacket that he always wears.'

'That's the standard chef outfit.'

'But he doesn't wear it when he's on Jonathan Ross. He just wears jeans and a tee-shirt which makes him look like those smelly people who sleep on the pavements and are always asking me for money. Mum gives them some coins but I always ask them if I could have them back so I can get a few packets of Love Hearts but they never hand me the dosh – the greedy bastards.'

As I'm now jobless I cannot afford to go to one of London's most expensive restaurants and it's a massive risk taking Sam out socially, but my hope is that Sam will enjoy the experience and perhaps soften his attitude to me.

Or is that just wishful thinking?

CHAPTER FOURTEEN

'Can I help you sir?' A tall, posh man, dressed in a suit, asks me as we enter the restaurant.

'Have you got any tables available for tonight?'

'Normally you have to book three months in advance but we've had a few cancellations today due to a rather high profile soccer match.'

That'll be England playing in a World Cup qualifying match. I was going to watch as well. Never mind.

'Follow me sir.'

I look around at the other diners and they are all dressed as if they're going to meet the Queen at Buckingham Palace. I'm in jeans and Sam's still in his school uniform.

'Can I get a photo with that Simmonds fella? You know the bloke in the white jacket who swears a lot.'

'Chef Simmonds is here tonight. I shall ask him to pop over.'

'I don't want to see him if he's dressed like a tramp. He has to have his white jacket on.'

'As he's helping preparing the food tonight I'm sure he'll have his chef jacket on.'

The waiter hands us both the menus and I'm shocked to see how much this is going to cost. Each meal is one hundred and sixty pounds so with the tip that'll set me back three hundred and fifty quid.

'Is there anything on the menu you like?' I ask Sam. 'We can still go to Wetherspoons. They do great chips.'

'I want to try the duck. They make me laugh.'

Oh well, I tried.

'Are you ready to order?' The waiter asks a short time later.

'For the starters can I have a duck? But I don't want to eat the beak. It'll hurt my teeth.'

The waiter looks confused; totally understandable.

'He's autistic,' I say to him. He nods and smiles back at me.

'For dinner I'll have that roast pigeon. Do you go to Trafalgar Square to get them? I sometimes go there with Mum and chase after them but they always fly away. Your cooks must be very fast to catch them.'

'I'll have the spring salad for starters and lamb for the main,' I tell the waiter before he has a chance to reply to Sam.

'And don't forget to leave out the beak,' Sam shouts to the waiter as he's walking away.

Twenty minutes later Sam takes the first bite of his duck and immediately spits it out.

'This food is shit.'

I suspect they won't be using that line to promote this restaurant.

'What's the matter with it?' I ask.

'It makes me want to puke up.'

That's another line that won't be used.

'Don't worry, I'm sure you'll like the pigeon,' I reply with zero confidence.

'That Simmonds bloke is a liar. He tells everyone he's a cook but he can't be. Is he just saying that to get on TV?'

'No, Gordon Simmonds is one of the top chefs in the world.'

'Nonsense.'

Soon after finishing my salad the waiter brings Sam's roast pigeon and my lamb.

'I thought that the pigeon was supposed to be grey and where are the wings?' Sam informs me.

'Just taste it,' I tell him.

Sam takes a bite and not surprisingly spits it out again.

'That can't be a Trafalgar Square pigeon, they're all nice and friendly'.

'Is there a problem?' The waiter asks.

'Where's that Simmonds geezer?'

Suddenly Gordon Simmonds approaches our table.

'Can I help you?' He asks the both of us.

'Are you really a cook or just an actor pretending to be a cook?' Sam asks.

'Yes, I am a cook. I currently have seven Michelin star restaurants and have had seventeen in total. I hope that answers your question,' he replies smiling, although I can tell he's a little agitated.

'I don't know what you're banging on about. This is not a Trafalgar Square pigeon and where are the wings?'

Simmonds looks at Sam and then at me. I think he's waiting for a punchline.

'I'm sorry, Sam's autistic. He wasn't too keen on the duck and the pigeon,' I explain.

He immediately relaxes.

'So, Sam, what would you like instead? We'll make you anything.'

'Chips and steak and kidney pie.'

'That's no problem. In fact I'll make it myself.'

'Don't cock it up.'

'I'll do my best. Is there anything else I can do for you?'

'Because you're wearing the white jacket I'd like to have my photo with you but don't you dare put your arm around me cos that'll make me cry.'

A bemused Gordon Simmonds kindly poses for a socially distanced photo with Sam and I also get a selfie with him.

One hundred and sixty pounds for chips and steak and kidney pie must be an entry for the Guinness Book Of Records, but Sam loved it and we both got photos with Gordon Simmonds so I'll worry about my depleted bank balance in the morning.

CHAPTER FIFTEEN

'I can't wait to show Dad the white jacket photo,' Sam tells me on the car journey home.

'You mean the photo with you and Gordon Simmonds?'

'Yeah. His steak and kidney pie was even better than the Sainsbury's one. Can we go there again tomorrow?'

'No, I don't think so.'

'Why not?'

'It's very expensive. We can go to McDonalds or Wetherspoons though.'

'Just ask the bank for more notes and coins. They have loads of them in their buildings and they always smile when they hand the money to Mum. They just love giving away their notes.'

It's not quite as simple as that.

My promotion of McDonalds or Wetherspoons doesn't appear to be working.

'You have to sleep on the sofa tonight. I don't want you upstairs at all,' Sam informs me soon after our arrival 'home'.

'Why's that?'

'I don't want strangers near me at night. I couldn't sleep yesterday because you were in Mum's bed and

I thought you'd be dancing in the landing all night long.'

'I don't usually dance too much in the middle of the night. Anyway I'm not a stranger now, I'm your mum's friend and hopefully I'm your friend now.'

'Mum and Dad are my friends, nobody else.'

'OK, but did you have a nice evening with me?'

'It wasn't crap but only because the pie was delicious.'

So it seems the only way I can gain any sort of affection from him is to take him to Gordon's every night. I feel disappointed that he still doesn't trust me. It hurts more than I thought it would.

'OK, I'll sleep downstairs. Get a good night's sleep and don't forget to brush your teeth.'

'I brush seven times a day and at night I always count my teeth just to make sure I haven't lost any. At the moment I've got twenty-six.'

'That's good to hear.'

With that he makes his way upstairs. There are still a couple of beers in the fridge so I help myself to one. It's much needed. Where do I go from here?

It's obvious Karen doesn't have someone to look after Sam. Social Services is a possibility but she's clearly reluctant to pursue that given her past experiences. The only other option is Rob. He's a selfish arsehole but he's Sam's father and I think he should know about Karen's accident and have the opportunity to look after his son. Why is she so reluctant to let this happen and putting all her trust in me when I have zero parental experience and know nothing about autism? Sam's behaviours are bewildering to me. I just can't predict what he's going to say or do next and I find this extremely unnerving.

I feel trapped but how can I possibly leave now?

I need to focus on getting my CV updated and contacting employment agencies. As soon as I drop Sam off at school tomorrow I'll make this my top priority.

My thoughts turn to Maria as I've really landed her in it, although that wasn't my intention – Peter can take responsibility for that.

I dial her number.

'Maria, how are you doing?'

'I'm still at the office trying to get on top of things.'

'I'm so sorry for all of this. I feel terrible.'

'You did what you thought was the right thing to do. It's not your fault that our boss is an arrogant piece of shit. I always suspected he was but you shielded his worst behaviours from me. Now I'm experiencing him first hand. Anyway let's not waste any more time talking about him. How's Karen?'

'She's doing OK but probably won't be released from the hospital for at least a couple of days.'

'And you're still looking after Sam?'

'Yeah, not much has changed on that front since we last spoke but I've just had an idea. I've got my work laptop with me so if you email me your implementation plan and what programs need coding I'll make a start on them. I've not much else to do and officially I'm still employed by *FixIT* for the next couple of weeks. But don't tell he who must be obeyed.'

'Haven't you got enough on your plate right now?'

'When I drop Sam off at school tomorrow I'm free for the rest of the day. The only thing I do need to do is update my CV and get it out there. But I can only work when I'm not with Sam. Right now he's in bed.'

'That's going to be a game changer. As you know so much about the project there's no handover required, which was going to be the time consuming part of this. Are you absolutely sure?'

'Yes, of course and I'll put your name on all my programs. You might even get the bonus if we can pull this off.'

'I know why Karen has more faith in you looking after her son than his father. You're reliable, kind and thoughtful. You've made my day.'

'OK, don't get all soppy with me. Just send over the plan and I'll start working on it tonight.'

'When you're finished looking after Sam and we make good headway on the project I'd like to take you out for a meal.'

'There's really no need.'

'Yes there is. You've been treated so badly but you still want to see the project through. I'd like to show you how much I appreciate your help.'

'I'll look forward to that, as long as it's not at Gordon Simmond's restaurant.'

'Are you kidding? I'm not that grateful.'

I finally shut down my work laptop at one-thirty in the morning feeling confident that between us we'll be able to meet the project deadlines. I also feel good about helping Maria, knowing that she will get the credit for all of this.

Plus another night out with Maria is an added incentive to crack on with this damn IT project but I really need to push Karen to find someone else to look after Sam. There must be somebody?

With all the uncertainty of the last forty-eight hours I'm happy to be doing something that I'm comfortable with.

It's also a welcome distraction from looking after a boy who doesn't like eating pigeons or ducks and was actually rude to the formidable Gordon Simmonds.

CHAPTER SIXTEEN

'Do you like mailboxes?'

I'm laying on the sofa half asleep. Sam is sitting in the armchair opposite me. He's fully dressed and looks ready for school.

'What time is it?' I ask.

'Seventeen minutes past five. Do you like mailboxes?'

'They're OK I suppose.'

'So you don't really like them?'

'No, they're great,' I reply, not wanting to get him in an agitated mood about saying anything negative about mailboxes.

'I love licking them. They taste better than some of Mum's dinners. Have you ever licked them?'

'Not recently.'

'The ones in Brixton are the best but I'd love to visit America so I can taste their ones. I bet they're fantastic.'

'Apart from mailboxes what else do you like about America?'

'In their diners you pay for one coffee and they give you loads of other coffees for free. I'd stay in there all day drinking coffee.'

'I didn't know you liked coffee?'

'I don't.'

'That's good that you like American mailboxes and having access to coffee, even though you don't like it. Anything else?'

'Pancakes with syrup, cowboys, yellow taxis, President Biden's hair and their mountains.'

Not all obvious choices but it's subjective.

'What do you think about pavements?'

'They're great.' I'm learning quickly.

'Even the ones that are loose and make you fall over?'

'No, they're not great.'

'I bet the American pavements aren't loose. They call them sidewalks, isn't that a much better name?'

'Yes it certainly is.'

'They look bigger which means people don't bump into each other all the time. I hate it whenever anyone touches me.'

'Why's that?'

'It gives me a headache.'

'Don't you like it when your mum touches you?'

'She's the only person in the world who doesn't give me a headache. She must have special powers.'

'And what about your dad?'

'He never touches me.'

'Doesn't he ever kiss you?'

'Yes, he did kiss me on the nineteenth of April two thousand and nineteen. Mum gave me a paracetamol afterwards.'

Wow, Rob not kissing his son for nearly four years – what a father!

'Do you want Rice Krispies for breakfast?' I ask.

'Yes, but I've already packed the Rice Krispies in my bag and I'll take the milk out of the fridge just before we go. I want the school to make it.'

'I can do it now. It'll save you carrying it.'

'No, my teacher said that I can leave the Rice Krispies and milk at the school for the whole week. They're experts at making my breakfast.'

He still doesn't trust me.

I drop Sam at school and head to my place where I pack a suitcase of clothes to bring to Karen's. Any hopes I had of escaping from this situation are rapidly diminishingly.

My thoughts turn to my employment status. I still can't believe that I'm out of work in such unfair circumstances.

I am on friendly terms with Jerry, who is the head of Human Resources at *FixIt*, so I arrange to meet him in a coffee bar near the Holborn office.

'I was surprised to hear you're no longer with us,' Jerry says, handing me a cappuccino.

'That's what I wanted to talk to you about. It's a long story but I'll keep it brief. My ex-wife had a road accident a few days ago and I'm looking after her autistic son while she's in hospital. She's got a broken hip and will need a long recovery period. She's not with the father, who is a complete waste of space so that's why I'm involved.'

'I didn't even know that you were married?'

'I've been divorced a long time. Anyway I couldn't attend this really important meeting with our American clients because I had to take the boy to school and straight away Peter took me off the project and is not renewing my contract. Now I know full well that as a consultant this sort of thing can happen but I wondered if there's any grounds to appeal? I just think it's so unfair.'

'How long was left of your contract?'

'Just over two weeks.'

'I'm sure you know this already but as a consultant you haven't got much protection, that's why they pay you much more than the permanent employees. I've seen termination of contracts for much less than what you've just told me, so there's not much you can do. Given your experience and qualifications though I don't think you'll have much trouble finding another position.'

'That's what I'd thought you'd say.'

'I wish I could give you a more positive answer but in my opinion I think it's a waste of time to appeal. I've yet to see a successful one in these circumstances. It's a ruthless business.'

'No worries, Jerry. Thanks for taking the time to talk to me.'

As soon as I arrive back at Karen's I update my CV and email it to a couple of employment agencies. Within an hour one of them contacts me and I arrange to pop into their office in Victoria.

It's a very plush office and nearly all the staff look like teenagers. Suddenly I feel very old.

'You're an experienced analyst but between you and me employers are mainly looking for graduates. They're cheaper and I see that you were on quite a high salary at *FixIT*,' one of the teenagers tells me.

'That's because I was on a short term contract as a consultant. I don't mind taking a permanent position – needs must.'

'Why are you leaving *FixIT*?'

'I fancied a new challenge.'

Does he believe my bullshit?

'What's your availability?'

'I can start pretty much straight away.' That's not strictly true given the Sam situation but I have to show willing.

'Do you have any hobbies?'

'Is that relevant?'

'IT employers these days like to know more about the person rather than just their skills.'

'I like reading.'

'Anything else? Sports?'

'Football, maybe tennis. I work long hours which doesn't leave much time for hobbies.'

I'm really not projecting a dynamic personality. More like the nerdy, boring type which is the norm in IT.

'Well thanks for coming along. It was great to meet you and we'll be in touch should any suitable positions come up.'

I can tell from the look in his eyes that this is a standard line that he probably says several times a day. I shake his hand and leave the teenagers to debate which nightclub they'll be frequenting tonight.

I didn't know what to expect at the employment agency but I thought that at the very least he would have shown an element of interest even if he was just paying lip service. He was basically saying that at forty I'm too old and too expensive to hire. I hope I'm wrong but I doubt it. I head back to Brixton with my suitcase full of clothes, more depressed than ever.

As I approach Karen's house I can see a man sitting on the front door step and as I get nearer I recognise him. It's Rob.

CHAPTER SEVENTEEN

'We meet again,' I say.

'Sam texted me – the message was a bit garbled but he seems to think that Karen's in hospital and you're looking after him? What's going on?' Rob replies.

'Let's not discuss this out here, shall we go inside?' He nods.

'Why are you staying here with my son?' He asks as we enter the living-room.

'On Sunday we all went to London...'

'You, Karen and Sam?'

'Yes.'

'Are you getting back with Karen?'

'No, not that it's any business of yours. When we were in London Sam ran into the road but Karen managed to pull him back onto the pavement. Unfortunately she got hit by a car and is in hospital with a broken hip.'

'Why didn't she tell me? I should be looking after Sam.'

'Nothing to do with me, that's Karen's decision but I suspect it's down to the fact that she doesn't trust you to look after him.'

'She's just being controlling; getting her own back.'

'Why is she so pissed off with you? Is it something to do with you shagging other women when you were married to her?'

'Spare me the sarcasm.'

'Karen doesn't want you anywhere near Sam and I don't blame her. From what she tells me you hardly see him from one month to the next. Why do you care all of a sudden?'

'She won't be physically able to look after him, so I'm taking control now. I'm going to the school and I'll be taking him home with me. I'm his father and you're incapable of looking after him. It's as simple as that.'

'To think we were once friends and I helped you out with your school work. More fool me.'

'I used you. I was never any good academically and you were stupid enough to do my homework for me. It freed me up to chase girls.'

'Your favourite hobby.'

'It still is. I managed to screw your wife and ruin your marriage, remember? There was a certain satisfaction in doing that.'

'Did you deliberately go with Karen because of me? What did I ever do to you apart from helping you out at school whenever you asked me to?'

'I couldn't believe how you could bag Karen. I mean you're hardly Brad Pitt. I tried to get off with her during the early part of your relationship but she was besotted with you. That was a mystery to me. But then you were barely at home, gallivanting around the country with your stupid job, so I took my chance. Karen was ripe for picking. She was lonely and I showed her a lot of attention and she caved in. I must admit she was very adventurous in the bedroom.'

I want to punch his arrogant face but what good will that do? I take a moment to compose myself.

'You really are a nasty piece of work, Rob. You were always a bit of a Jack the Lad, but fun to be with. What changed to make you so bitter and angry?'

'I'm in no mood for your psychological claptrap. I'm going to gather up Sam's clothes.'

'In case you're interested, Karen had the hip operation and it was successful. The doctor said that she will make a full recovery and as soon as she's home and mobile enough she'll be picking up Sam, rest assured on that.'

'We'll see,' he replies.

With that he heads upstairs. Unfortunately, as he's Sam's father there's not a damn thing I can do to stop him. Karen is going to be distraught at this latest development. She hid Sam's mobile in one of her bedroom drawers so he must have found it either last night or this morning and texted his father. I know Rob still works for his dad's building company so I'm assuming he'll be able to take time off to do the school run. Rob's father Alex, from what I remember, is a completely different character to his son. He's friendly, kind and funny. Whenever I went to Rob's house he always took the time to have a chat with me. Karen told me that he's still working even though he must be in his early seventies now. She really liked Alex. Maybe he could be the voice of reason in all this madness?

Ten minutes later Rob appears carrying a holdall.

'I'll leave you to your little love nest. Good luck explaining this to Karen,' he says, smiling.

Why is he so bitter? Is it the fact that Karen found out that he was cheating on her and was strong enough to chuck him out and divorce him? He obviously hates not having the upper hand. From what Karen told me Rob stayed at his parents for a couple of months before renting a one bedroom flat in Balham. That must have hurt. It sounds like he didn't do particularly well out of the divorce settlement either. Karen also said that his parents gave him the down payment for his Streatham flat but apparently his mortgage is huge. It's likely he's struggling financially.

Maybe he should have paid more attention at school and not relied on me.

As their divorce was only finalised a few months ago it's obviously all still raw for him.

Now all I have to do is tell Karen the news she will not be wanting to hear.

CHAPTER EIGHTEEN

'Where's Sam?' Karen asks me as I enter her room at the hospital.

'When I arrived at your house Rob was waiting for me…'

'Please don't tell me he's taken Sam.'

'I'm afraid he has.'

'Why didn't you stop him?'

'How could I? He's his father.'

'I can't believe this is happening. How did he find out?'

'Sam found his mobile and texted him.'

'Is he staying at Rob's or with Rob's parents?'

'I don't know, he didn't say.'

'I've got to get my boy back now,' she makes an attempt to get out of bed but winces in pain and decides against it.

'Karen, calm down. You're not fit enough to leave. You can't risk it. Just let him stay with Rob tonight and we'll see how things go tomorrow. Did the doctor give you any indication when you can leave?'

'He's going to examine me again in the morning and make a decision then. He did say that the hip is healing but slower than he originally thought. I've got a feeling he's going to say I need to stay here longer.'

'Unfortunately that's out of your hands and I can't take Sam away from his father – I'll be arrested if I do.'

'But he's totally irresponsible. I don't trust him to look after my son. You don't know what he's like. He's using Sam to get back at me. He's evil.'

'I know this is not good but what's the worst that can happen? Please don't worry too much. Just try to be patient, hopefully you won't be in here too much longer.'

'No, there is something we can do – get in touch with Alex and Nora.'

'Rob's parents? But how can they help?'

'They've always been nice to me. Alex has told me on several occasions that Rob doesn't deserve me. If they knew how concerned I was I'm sure they would offer to look after Sam for a day or two.'

'But how is that any different from your own parents looking after Sam?'

'His parents are a bit younger and more physically and mentally up to it, especially Alex.'

'OK, I'll give them a ring if you feel that might work.'

'I don't have their number. I never did. Rob did all the arranging whenever we visited them, so Danny...'

'Will I go around their place to ask them to reason with their son?' I interrupt.

'I know it's asking a lot yet again and you've done so much for me in the last forty-eight hours but please can you visit them? You know they'll be delighted to see you.'

'Will they? When I tell them that their son is not capable of looking after their grandchild? I'm sure they won't be too thrilled to hear that.'

'There's something else.'

'What?'

'As you've already witnessed Rob has a temper and there have been a few occasions when he got so angry with Sam that I thought he was going to hit him but he just managed to control himself enough not to. But he threw Sam's toys against the TV once and smashed the screen. Rob also broke his own finger when he smashed his fist so hard on the living-room door after Sam did something that agitated him.'

'But he's never actually hit him?'

'No, but he's never looked after him on his own. I know he won't cope and I'm scared what he might do to Sam.'

'OK, enough said, I'll do it. Do they still live on Stanley Road?'

She nods and starts to cry. I gently put an arm around her and she holds on to me tightly. This instantly brings me back to happier times in our relationship.

Back then I thought that Karen was just perfect – beautiful, great sense of humour, kind, caring and self-deprecating. If I hadn't asked her to marry me I just knew I'd regret it for the rest of my life.

The day before I was going to pop the question I was chatting with my mum and she asked how I was getting on with Karen. Although I had no intention of letting her in on my proposal plans I suddenly blurted it out. 'Don't you think you're punching above your weight?' was her immediate reply. That didn't exactly calm my nerves. 'She's a lovely girl but she could marry Hugh Grant if she wanted to.' I wasn't aware that she knew Hugh Grant? My mum wasn't intentionally nasty, she just had no filter. 'We get on great. I'm confident she'll say yes,' I told her. 'I don't think she will, but I wish you the best of luck anyway,' was her reply.

The following night Karen and I went to a South Kensington restaurant. When the waitress served the soup I got down on one knee but my head knocked one of the bowls out of her hand and the soup went all over me and the waitress. Luckily it was lukewarm but with half a bowl of tomato soup on my shirt I still asked Karen to marry me. She was thrilled to bits and said 'yes'. Some of the diners clapped and a few took photos which they sent to us. We always laughed looking at those photos with my white and tomato red shirt. The manager of the restaurant even paid for our meal and gave me a clean shirt to wear on our special night. It was the happiest day of my life.

When I rang Mum later to tell her my news she said 'I'm pleased for you, Danny but I don't know what's in it for her.' I wasn't particularly happy with that remark but today I manage to smile at the memory – thanks, Mum! Luckily Karen doesn't see my expression.

CHAPTER NINETEEN

Karen was more hopeful of a positive outcome after I agreed to meet Alex and Nora. But how am I going to approach this? It's not going to be easy.

A few days ago my life was a lot simpler than it is right now.

Outside of work my life is insular. Over a weekend I virtually see no-one, apart from the local supermarket staff. Am I turning into a sad, lonely man?

The friends that I once shared with Karen have disappeared over the years but that was mainly down to me. After our divorce I felt awkward seeing these happily married couples with 2.4 children. So what did I do? I declined their social invitations to the point where I wasn't asked anymore. It was a relief for me and no doubt them too.

Occasionally I got a text asking how I was doing and suggesting we should meet up for a drink. It never happened.

Since Christmas Day I've suddenly being thrown into a family life situation, albeit a messy one that involves my ex-wife, her ex-husband and an eleven-year-old autistic boy.

Has this temporary lifestyle change made me imagine what might have been? Yes, of course, but most of the time I long to return to my solitary life.

The positive side of all this is reconnecting with Karen. Despite the bitterness I carried with me for so many years after our divorce I now feel an affection for her again. She made a mistake, owned it and has had to live with it. On the day of the accident I was going to draw a line on maintaining any sort of relationship with her, and of course Sam. Do I still feel the same? I honestly don't know.

An hour after leaving the hospital I'm standing outside Alex and Nora's house in Stockwell. It must be twenty-five years since I've seen them.

I spent many evenings at this house helping Rob with his school work and usually staying for dinner. They were always grateful to me for taking the time to help their son. They even bought me presents to show their appreciation. I just hope the goodwill that I built up all those years ago will stand me in good stead now.

I have no idea what their reaction will be to Karen's suggestion but there's only one way to find out. I ring the bell.

'Well, well, well, long time no see. Please come in, Danny.' Alex says.

As I enter the hallway he shakes my hand. Naturally he looks older, more grey hairs and a bit thicker around the waist but overall in pretty good shape for a man of his age.

As I enter the living-room Nora slowly rises up from her armchair and gives me a hug. In contrast with Alex she looks thinner and more frail but still has that welcoming smile I remember so well.

So far so good.

'What a lovely surprise,' Nora says.

'Do you want a cup of tea?' Alex inquires.

'No, thanks. I'm sorry to barge in on you like this but I've got a big favour to ask.'

'Go on,' Alex says.

'I'm not sure if you know but Karen's in hospital right now, she got hit by a car.'

'Oh my God, is she OK?' Nora asks.

'She's got a broken hip and has already had the operation. It's just going to take some time for her to recover.'

'Rob never told us about this. When did it happen?' Alex asks.

'On Sunday but Rob only found out today. This afternoon he's picking Sam up from school.'

They both look concerned.

'This is really awkward for me to say but Karen doesn't want Rob looking after Sam while she's in hospital and that's the reason why I've been looking after him the last couple of days.'

'Are you and Karen back together?' Nora inquires.

'No, we were in contact on Facebook over Christmas and have met a few times since. We're just catching up a bit, that's all.'

'Why doesn't Karen want Rob to look after Sam?' Alex asks.

'She thinks he won't be able to cope. She says Rob doesn't see Sam that often and when he does it's very brief. Karen wants to know if you could persuade Rob to bring Sam here for a couple of days so you could look after him until she gets out of hospital. She's worried about his safety.'

'What do you mean?' Alex asks, staring at me. Having already had a confrontation with Rob earlier, I'm not in the mood for another one with his father.

'I understand there have been a number of incidents where Rob has lost his temper with Sam and although he's never physically hurt him Karen is concerned that his anger might get the better of him.'

'And hurt Sam?' Nora asks.

I nod.

Alex and Nora look at each other but don't speak for what seems like an eternity.

'Danny, as painful as it is to hear that, we understand Karen's anxiety but knowing Rob, as we all do, do you really think that we could persuade him to let Sam stay with us? If he did, we'd gladly have our grandson here for however long is required but Rob's his own man and doesn't take advice from anybody and I mean anybody. But what I will do is go over to Rob's shortly and make sure everything is OK. I can't do any more than that. I'm sorry,' Alex says.

'We'll try to see Sam as often as we can while Karen's in hospital. We've hardly seen him in the past year so we'll be delighted to spend some time with him. Please tell Karen not to worry, we'll keep an eye on him,' Nora adds.

'Thanks for being so understanding, I really appreciate it.'

'Don't worry, Danny, nothing you said has shocked us. We know all too well what Rob's like,' Nora says.

We spend the next hour recalling old times. They both seem to have almost total recall and tell me stories that I have long forgotten. It was wonderful to catch up with them.

They are such decent people, which begs the question how did it all go so wrong with Rob?

I make my way back to the hospital to relay the news to Karen, hoping she'll be happy with this solution but somehow I don't think she will be.

CHAPTER TWENTY (ROB)

'Do you like the sky?' Sam asks.

'What do you mean?' I reply.

'The sky above your head. What do you think of it?'

'I really don't give a toss.'

'Has America got the same sky as England?'

'The sky is in every country.'

'There's loads of Brixton clouds but I don't see clouds in any of the American films. Why's that?'

'Please stop asking me these stupid questions and let me concentrate on the driving, OK?'

I only picked up Sam less than ten minutes ago and he's already irritating the fuck out of me. I know that he has special needs and I should be more patient with him but I've yet to have a half decent conversation with my son and there's no sign of that changing anytime soon. I mean what do they teach him at school? Encouraging meaningless drivel about the sky?

My mind drifts back to the day Sam was born. We didn't want to know the sex of the baby but secretly I was desperate to have a son, someone to carry on the family name. PS that isn't going to happen.

The first couple of years after Sam was born were great. We did everything together as a family and I even remained faithful to Karen during this period, but the autistic diagnosis changed everything. I didn't understand how that could have happened. I still can't. We were asked by an autistic consultant if there were any family members who suffer from depression, alcoholism or any sort of mental or neurological disorders. They also wanted to know if anyone was eccentric or routine driven, but I think most families have someone that fit into one or more of these categories. So why were we dealt the autistic card? It drove me crazy thinking about it. Karen was much more practical and although she was deeply upset when we got the news about Sam, she coped with it much better than me. I started drinking more and rekindled my lust for women. I didn't care if they were single or married. If they were willing then so was I. These affairs continued for a few years and I really thought that I was being ultra-careful in covering my tracks, but obviously not. Karen eventually found out and took me to the cleaners with the divorce. She hired a couple of really expensive lawyers who did their job extremely well. I underestimated her determination to see it through. I was convinced that she was going to change her mind. I asked her several times how she could afford to get those guys but she never told me. I suspect her parents helped her out because they really didn't care for me at all. I wasn't good enough for their precious daughter.

So here I am taking my son back to my two bedroom flat in Streatham. What the hell am I going to do with him? I've no idea what his interests are, apart from playing with ants. What's all that about?

Karen will be spitting blood when she finds out that I have Sam and that's the sole reason why I'm doing this. That bitch ruined my life when she took virtually every penny that I have; now it's payback time.

I would just love to be a fly on the wall when that gormless arsehole Danny tells her the news.

'Do they have zebra crossings in Streatham?' Sam asks.

'Of course they do.'

'I don't like them.'

'OK, whatever.'

'I hate walking on the white bits so I always jump over them. Do you do that as well?'

'No, Sam, I don't do that,' I reply, trying but failing not to sound both bored and pissed off. Not that he'd notice.

'That stranger man wore your underpants.'

'What are you talking about?'

'That stranger that stayed in my house while Mum was having a lie in at that hospital building.'

'Danny wore my underpants?'

'Yes and Mum's knickers as well.'

Either Danny has turned into a pervert or, as I suspect, Sam is talking complete nonsense as usual.

'Are you looking forward to going to Daddy's flat?' I ask. This will be his first visit there.

'No.'

'Why's that?'

'Because the carpet will be different from my house. That worries me.'

'For Christ's Sake – carpets are nothing to get hung up about. You've really got to snap out of these weird obsessions. I don't want to hear about this shit again, OK?'

'Have you got just plain carpets or have they got patterns on them?'

'What did I just say?'

'I have to know before I go into the flat.'

'No you don't.'

'Please tell me what colour your carpets are and if they have any patterns?'

'No, I won't. You can't go through life getting worked up about bullshit.'

Sam starts crying and it's not a temper tantrum, it's a scared cry. He's afraid, but of what? Fucking carpets. This is just madness. The crying is getting louder and is doing my head in.

'OK, OK, all the carpets are plain, no patterns. In the living-room the carpet is grey, it's dark green on the stairs and sky blue in the bedroom that you'll be sleeping in tonight. Does that satisfy you?'

He nods.

I gave in too easily but he's clearly distressed. This shit is much deeper than I thought. Of course I should anticipate his reaction, but to be honest I hardly know my own son. When we were all together I didn't see a lot of him. I worked long hours and spent the weekends usually playing golf and then socialising afterwards. I have witnessed many of his autistic behavioural traits over the years but whenever there was anything too serious I left it for Karen to deal with. She was always telling me about his episodes but it went in one ear and out the other. I wasn't interested. I know that makes me sound like an awful father but I just couldn't handle it. I want my son to be normal but he isn't and never will be. If anything, his autistic behaviours are now more pronounced, as I've just witnessed.

'What do you want for dinner?' I ask Sam.

'Is there a Sainsbury's in Streatham?'

'Yes.'

'What food have they got in Sainsbury's?'

'They have everything.'

'Do they have beans?'

'Yes.'

'What about butter?'

'Yes, of course.'

'I like Coca Cola, do they have that as well?'

'Sam, I'm not going through every single product in Sainsbury's, just tell me what you want.'

'Do they have Coca Cola?'

'Yes, every food shop in the world has Coca Cola.'

'But I only like it in cans. I don't like the bottles cos they slip out of my hands and smash everywhere. The bottles frighten me.'

'I'm pretty sure they have cans.'

'I think you should ring them and find out. The smashed glass hurts my ears and makes me cry.'

At this point I feel like returning to Brixton to hand Sam back. He's a fucking nightmare. This is like Chinese torture. It's no wonder I completely withdrew from my parental responsibilities. What does a father discuss with a normal eleven-year-old boy? Probably football, music, TV, maybe even girls, whereas I'm being pressurised to contacting Sainsbury's to make sure that they stock Coca Cola cans rather than bottles because my son is afraid of them. This just about sums up Sam's life.

My friends, who have children, tell me that I should be more considerate of Sam's needs but they haven't got a clue what it's like living with an autistic child. They all think I'm a very confident, even an arrogant, person, but when it comes to Sam I'm absolutely clueless. You would think by now that I'd be used to his strange ways but I'm not.

Occasionally I do think about Sam's future – what sort of a life will he lead? As far as I know he hasn't got too many friends and the ones he does have are also autistic – I can only imagine the types of conversations that they have.

Do I feel guilty that I've let Karen carry the burden of looking after Sam? Yes, I do sometimes, but not often. My life is much simpler these days. I can come and go as I please with little responsibilities, although in truth I should have more responsibility than most parents, but I opted out of all of that.

I wanted to have children, I really did. We planned for at least two but that changed with the autistic diagnosis. That day changed my life. We both knew that Sam was behind his peers, both verbally and more importantly with his strange behaviour. He rarely looked at us when we were talking to him. When there was a family gathering he just played with his toys on his own, he never engaged with his cousins at all. He used to regularly wake up at some ridiculous hour in the morning and never wanted to go back to sleep. This meant that either myself or Karen had to take him downstairs to watch endless cartoons. This task usually fell to Karen although there were times when I looked after him and getting only two or three hours sleep made the day at work very tiring for me. It took its toll. Sleep deprivation makes me edgy and as Karen and myself were both in the same boat it led to many arguments. It was just so depressing as there just didn't seem an end in sight.

For the first couple of years in Sam's life I did my best to be a decent father. I think even Karen will agree on that, but the sleepless nights and Sam's bizarre behaviours really affected me, it got to the stage where I didn't want to spend any time with him; and consequently Karen.

After Karen found out about my affairs she packed my bags and told me to leave so I moved in with my parents. That was humiliating. Even though it was my own fault I resented her for putting me in that situation. That resentment increased with the expense of the divorce, which virtually ruined me. I never thought Karen would be that ruthless and I hated her for it.

The friends we had sided with her. Soon after our split I never heard from most of them again. I was portrayed as the bad guy in all of this. Nobody understood the pressure I was under every single day trying to look after a special needs child. I wonder how many of our so called friends' marriages would have also suffered if they were in the same situation?

Mum and Dad really liked Karen and were so despondent when all of this happened. They knew that it was all my fault but they never pointed the finger of blame at me. They supported me financially and emotionally and I'll never forget that.

So why am I not more involved in Sam's life? It's just too much responsibility. It's got to be all or nothing and I chose nothing.

Ten minutes later we're in Sainsbury's.

'This is the fifth Sainsbury's that I've visited. I've been to the Brixton one, Stockwell, Norbury and Waterloo. The Waterloo store was too cramped and everyone kept barging into me, so Mum had to take me out as I was crying.'

'You were distressed because people were bumping into you?'

'Yes, it's just disgusting and I wanted to vomit.'

'Let me tell you something you'll get nowhere in life if you get upset about idiotic things like that. You've got to chill out.'

'I don't want to chill out.'

'Yeah, that much I do know.'

'Excuse me Sainsbury's man, do you have pasta sauce?' Sam asks a staff member.

'Yes, they're in aisle seven, do you want me to show you?'

'Do I have to walk alongside you or just a few steps behind?'

'Whatever you prefer.'

'I'll walk five steps behind. I don't want to get too close to you.'

I follow them both to the pasta aisle.

'As you can see we have tomato and basil sauce, tomato and herb...'

'That's enough. You can get lost now, I don't need you anymore.'

'I'm sorry, my son's autistic,' I tell the confused Sainsbury's guy.

He smiles and walks away. At least he's got an interesting anecdote to tell his colleagues on his break.

'That was rude,' I tell Sam.

'What was?'

'You told the man to get lost.'

'He was talking like a pasta madman. It was distracting.'

'OK, we're here now, do you want any of the pasta sauces?'

'No.'

'So what do you want?'

'I like looking at the different colours. They're amazing.'

After staring at the pasta sauces for a couple of minutes my patience is wearing a bit thin.

'Let's go now,' I say.

With that he starts to lick several of the pasta sauce jars. His saliva drips down the jars.

'What the fuck are you doing?' I say, as I wipe the jars with my shirt sleeve.

'But it tastes lovely.'

'Are you absolutely bonkers?' I shout at him. Several of the customers stare at me.

Sam then runs to the end of the aisle, kneels down and starts licking the floor. I catch up with him, grab his shirt collar in an attempt to pull him up.

'You're hurting me,' he yells.

'Get the fuck up now.'

'No, I need to clean the floor. It's dirty.'

'No, you don't,' I reply, attempting to haul him up again but it's impossible as he's a dead weight. In his struggle to get free from my grasp he hits his head on a plinth.

'What the hell's going on?' A security guy asks.

'My dad cracked my head open,' Sam replies holding the top of his head.

The security guy calls for back-up.

'It's not as bad as it looks. My son is autistic and started to lick the floor. I was trying to stop him,' I reply, sounding a bit too defensive.

He gently picks up Sam who co-operates. He looks at Sam's head and I can see a small trickle of blood.

Fuck.

'It was an accident...' I say, but he's looking doubtful.

Another male staff member arrives and ushers us into an office. The newcomer is a first aider.

'It's just a minor scratch. I'll put some antiseptic cream on it,' the first-aider explains.

A few minutes later a guy in a smart suit joins us.

'I've just looked at the CCTV footage and I can see you were just trying to lift him up, albeit in a somewhat heavy handed way,' the suited man tells me.

'He was licking the floor. I didn't want him to get ill.'

They look at me but don't respond. I get the impression that these jobsworths would like to take this further but I'm assuming the CCTV evidence is in my favour.

'Well, thanks for attending to Sam so promptly,' I say, although I really want to tell these smug interfering shits to get off their high horse and leave me be.

The suited man nods so I take it as my cue to leave.

'You've got a clean floor now on aisle seven. That makes me happy,' Sam tells them as we depart.

'What is the matter with you? You nearly got me into a lot of trouble,' I tell Sam on the way out of the store.

'Licking floors is one of my hobbies. Why did you stop me from having a fun time?'

'You could get ill from doing that.'

'That's ridiculous. I lick floors every day and I feel fine.'

'OK, let's just forget about it. If I take you to McDonalds will you just tell Mum that you fell over in Sainsbury's? She'll be upset if I stopped you from enjoying your hobby and we don't want to cause her any more stress, especially as she's not feeling well.'

'Does that mean I can have an extra sachet of tomato ketchup?'

'Yeah, why not?'

He's a tough negotiator.

Of course I'm talking utter bullshit. Sam is extremely vulnerable so I can tell him any old crap and he'll believe it. Karen will do her nut if she found out what actually happened and use that against me. OK, I barely see Sam from one month to the next but if Karen had her way she'll use this to further restrict my visits and gain greater control over my relationship with him. As I found out with the divorce she's extremely resourceful when need be. When I first started a relationship with her she was a much softer person but I suppose living with me all those years has toughened her up.

I knew that I used too much force when I grabbed his collar. I lost my temper. I kept telling him to stop, but he wouldn't. Some customers looked on in disgust when he was spitting on those jars and a few of them stopped and stared when he was licking the floor. Unfortunately the red mist descended on me, I overreacted.

Luckily Sam seems more upset about not completing his OCD rituals rather than being hurt, so I don't think he'll mention my involvement in his injury. I just hope that scratch on his head heals quickly.

I'm doing this just to piss off my ex-wife and get some control but is it worth it?

There is only one relationship in my life that I didn't end myself, so the answer is yes, it is definitely worth it. But as to how much longer I can tolerate this without completely losing my temper... I'm not sure.

CHAPTER TWENTY-ONE

'He's evil. Why is he suddenly so obsessed about caring for Sam when he's only seen him a handful of times since the divorce? He's not capable of looking after my son. He lost interest when Sam was about three. I want my son back now.'

'OK, Karen, calm down. Alex and Nora are popping over there this morning to check up on things. They'll make sure that Sam's OK.'

'I need to contact my solicitor. Rob hasn't paid me any child support for over two years – surely that alone has got to give me some leverage?'

'Sounds like a plan. Anyway, what's the latest medical update?' I ask.

'Bad news. It looks like I need another op as part of the hip may have been dislodged. I seem to remember him telling me this was a possibility when he was preparing me for the first operation.'

'Sorry to hear that. When will you know?'

'I'm having a scan later.'

'If you do have a second op do you know how much longer you'll have to stay here afterwards?'

'No. I suppose they'll have to wait and see how successful it is. I can't tell you how depressed I am over this and it's all my own fault. I should've been more focused with Sam on that busy road.'

'I distracted you, so please don't blame yourself. You're an amazing mother. I just don't know how you've coped on your own. I've only had a brief glimpse at your life and it's a real eye-opener.'

'Every time you come here, Danny you have to listen to me moaning. I'm really sorry. Your boss must be a very understanding guy to give you time off for these visits.'

'Yeah,' I reply, as it's definitely not the right time to tell Karen I've lost my job.

I leave Karen with the promise that I'll go and see Alex and Nora later after their visit to Rob.

With each passing day Karen is becoming increasingly distraught. The news that she'll probably be having another operation has not helped because she knows this will further delay her recovery. In addition, the situation with Rob looking after Sam is driving her crazy. I know that he was angry that I took care of Sam but I think his motives go beyond that. He doesn't really care for his son. Observing Rob when he unexpectedly turned up at Karen's house the other day, upsetting his son, was enough to convince me of that. He's doing it to cause Karen anxiety which is so cruel but of course Sam doesn't know any better. I doubt that even a normal eleven-year-old would understand.

Even though Sam hasn't exactly bonded with me I do feel protective towards him. Maybe this is due to the fact he's with Rob. I share Karen's anxiety over how Rob is treating him. The sooner I talk to Alex and Nora the better.

I wonder what my mother would make of all this? She would probably dismiss the autism diagnosis by saying something like 'he'll grow out of it.' She didn't care for Rob, often telling me 'he's just a show off.' That's just the tip of an iceberg. Dad was less opinionated and often told me to go with my gut feeling whenever I discussed a problem with him. Despite being very different personalities my parents had a happy marriage and I never told them about Karen's affair. They loved her so much. Even at the height of my bitterness towards Karen I still shielded her. Consequently, they never understood why our marriage ended. When they realised we weren't getting back together, Mum encouraged me to start dating again. 'Don't leave it too long cos all you'll end up with is a fat chav with a cigarette permanently dangling from her lips,' she said. I think that image put me off dating indefinitely.

After arriving home I start coding the IT programs for Maria. Between us we have made good progress and are on target to meet the deadlines. A night out with Maria is getting closer and the only thing I'm looking forward to right now.

A short time later I get a phone call from one of the employment agencies so I immediately make my way to Holborn, CV in hand.

I'm greeted by a young guy called Graham.

'Before we have a chat I'd like to give you an IT test if that's OK because I've spent many wasted hours interviewing clients who talk up their skills but then fail the technical test.'

'Of course, no problem,' I reply.

Graham hands me the test paper which consists of thirty questions. I go into a room and answer them all without too much difficulty.

Graham studies my answers and then smiles.

'One hundred percent. So let's talk. Why are you changing jobs?'

'The company I was with didn't renew my contract. Simple as that.' I've given up spouting the 'I wanted a new challenge' cliché answer.

'Why didn't they renew your contract?'

'I couldn't attend an important because my ex-wife was in hospital with a broken hip and I had to look after her son.'

'Wow. How is she?'

'She's recovering slowly but may need another operation.'

'I'm assuming you feel the decision to terminate your contract was harsh?'

'Absolutely, but my boss is a hard taskmaster so I wasn't totally surprised.'

'Well, Danny, I admire your honesty. I usually hear the same old clichés from clients, so your attitude is refreshing.'

'Does that stand me in good stead? I really need a job as I've got a lot of financial commitments.'

'Your IT skills are excellent but employers mostly prefer graduates. They're cheaper basically.'

Where have I heard that before?

'However, I'm confident that I'll succeed in getting you some interviews. I'm extremely resourceful.'

We chat for a while and I leave with a spring in my step. I'm hopeful Graham will utilise his over confident skills to line up some interviews for me.

These past few days have been stressful. Witnessing Karen's accident was horrific and I felt sick when I saw her motionless on the ground. For a moment I really thought she was dead. Looking after Sam has been life-changing. I can't predict what he's going to say or do, which leaves my nerves constantly on edge. I've barely slept the last few nights.

Then there's Rob. Trying to deal with his bitter attitude is difficult. He likes to be in total control and that hasn't happened in the past year or so. The fact that he's hardly paid Karen any child support doesn't surprise me. I'm guessing she gave up asking as no contact was probably a better option.

Not to forget, during all of this I lost my job. That trip to London with Karen and Sam really had a disastrous knock-on effect. However the employment agency interview has given me fresh hope. With this uplifting attitude I make my way to Alex and Nora.

'Did you get to see Sam?' I ask, after arriving at Alex and Nora's.

'Yes, we did,' Alex replies, nervously glancing at Nora.

'How is he?'

'He's got big since we last saw him and he's been telling us about his ant collection,' Nora replies.

'How was Rob with him?'

'He seemed agitated. He's never really looked after Sam on his own. As you know, Karen mostly took care of him. He snapped at Sam a couple of times,' Alex replies.

'Why?'

'Sam kept talking about Rob's carpets and furniture, so nothing much really. But there's something else...'

'Go on.'

'There's a big scratch on the top of his head, not deep but noticeable. Rob said that Sam fell over after running down an aisle in Sainsbury's and hit his head on a plinth.'

'Do you believe him?'

'I have to give him the benefit of the doubt,' Alex replies.

'Does that mean you're not totally convinced with Rob's explanation?'

'I wish I could say otherwise, but yes.'

'Karen's not going to be happy about this.'

'That's not all,' Alex says, 'we were leaving to go to his flat when they turned up here. Rob wants us to look after Sam.'

'Wow, that didn't last long but good news all the same. Where's Sam now?'

'He's in the garden. He's just walking up and down, talking to himself.'

I walk into the kitchen and through the window I see Sam looking up at the sky with great intensity. He's probably studying the Streatham cloud movements. He seems fascinated by clouds, which is just as well we live in this country where he'll be able to see plenty of them most days of the year.

I feel emotional just observing Sam. A parent's role should be to love and care for their children, even more so if they have special needs, but Rob has clearly decided to not get involved in his son's life, which I find so sad.

'I'll talk to Karen to see if she wants me to take him back home but that's taking nothing away from the both of you. I know that she completely trusts you both.'

'Rob told us in no uncertain terms not to hand Sam over to you,' Nora says.

'If Karen wanted to go down the legal route Rob wouldn't have a leg to stand on. The fact that Sam hurt himself in the short time Rob was with him doesn't do Rob any favours.'

'We don't know exactly what happened,' Alex says.

'Have you asked Sam?'

'Yes, he said it happened in Sainsbury's but wouldn't say any more.'

'I think it's probably best you speak to Karen about me taking Sam. I can ring her now.'

'There's no need. We've known you a long time. You're a good person and we know you only have Karen and Sam's best interests at heart. We'll deal with Rob.'

'If he doesn't want to look after his son why should he worry who does?' I ask.

'Maybe it's an ego thing. Rob struggled with fatherhood and dealing with Sam's special needs,' Alex replies.

'But he doesn't give the boy a chance. The moment Sam displays any of his autistic traits Rob loses it. He knows that Sam is different and will never be normal.'

'You would make a good father, Danny. We admire how you've helped Karen especially given the history between you both,' Nora says.

'You know what happened with us?'

'Yes, Rob told us one night after he had a few drinks. He seemed quite proud of it. We certainly weren't.'

'I've struggled with Sam so far but I'm willing to persist to help Karen.'

'Any chance you might get back together?'

'The answer is still no,' I reply, smiling.

I venture into the garden. Sam is on his knees digging up dirt with his hands. He looks up at me.

'Oh, shitting hell,' Sam says when he notices me.

'Hiya, Sam. I'm taking you back to your house.'

'Where's Dad?'

'He has to work.'

'Why did he buy that green sofa? It's ridiculous. And the water in his bathroom tap comes out too fast and splashes everywhere. His flat gave me a headache. If Dad promises not to bring his green sofa with him can he come back to my house now?'

'No, your father's staying in his flat.'

'Is it because he loves his furniture too much?'

'I don't think so.'

'Has he gone a bit mad?'

'No.'

Aggressive, self-centred, arrogant, egotistical – yes, but madness? Not yet, as far as I know.

CHAPTER TWENTY-TWO

As soon as we get back to Karen's I ring her.

'I've got Sam.'

'Wow, how did you manage that?'

'I went to Alex and Nora's and Sam was there. Rob had dropped him off earlier. Seems like he got fed up looking after him.'

'No surprise there. He barely lasted half a day.'

'He told Alex and Nora not to hand him over to me but thankfully they've got Sam's best interests at heart.'

'I can't believe it. Danny you're a lifesaver. I owe you big time.'

'Well you could've left a few more beers in the fridge.'

'That's a priority as soon as I get out of here. I've got some good news too...'

'Before you tell me I just want to say that Sam has a cut on his head. Rob told Alex and Nora that Sam fell over in Sainsbury's.'

'Oh God, how bad is it?'

'It's not deep, about two inches long.'

'How could that have happened?'

'I don't know. I haven't had a chance to grill Sam.'

'Do you think it's got anything to do with Rob?'

'Possibly but that may be unfair on Rob.'

'Is Sam OK?'

'He's fine. He didn't seem bothered by it. I'm sorry that we couldn't make it tonight but Alex and Nora wanted to spend some time with Sam but we'll come to see you after school tomorrow.'

'I can't wait.'

'Anyway, what's the news on another op?'

'I don't have to have one. It's such a relief.'

'That's wonderful. I know I seem to be asking this question continuously but do you have any idea when they will discharge you?'

'Hopefully tomorrow but I will still need help with Sam, at least until I'm more physically able.'

'I suppose I can stick around for a while if you want,' I say smiling.

'Are you sure?'

'No problem.'

'When Belinda comes back from the States she'll be able to help out, but until then…'

'Don't worry. Just get yourself better.'

Having Sam back and not needing another operation has really lifted Karen's spirits as well as the possibility of getting out of the hospital tomorrow. It's not the end of my involvement but it means that an end will soon be in sight; for me. The mention of Belinda possibly taking over is also another encouraging sign.

'Do Americans have shit days?' Sam asks me.

'Yes of course. Why do you ask that?'

'Because they're always saying have a nice day to everybody.'

'But sometimes they don't have nice days.'

'Then why don't they say have a nice or shitty day?'

I have no answer to that.

'You really do like America, don't you?' I ask him

'Yes, they smile more than the Brixton people and they never have any teeth missing.'

Two valid points.

In our first few days together he seemed reluctant to speak to me so I'm encouraged that he's beginning to open up more.

'If you don't mind me asking, Sam, have you got a girlfriend?'

'No way. All girls like pink and I hate pink so I'm not bothering with them.'

'You'll probably change your mind when you get older.'

'Nah. I see how long it takes Mum to put the make up on her face every day and I'm not wasting my time waiting around for all that shit.'

Maybe other single men are also adverse to the colour pink and the time consuming process of putting makeup on? Who knows?

Despite Sam's makeup protests I wonder what the chances are of him having a romantic relationship when he's older? Do autistic adults usually only date fellow autistic adults?

'So what happened when you fell over in Sainsbury's and cut your head?' I ask Sam.

'I like the flavour of the pasta sauce jars.'

'Did a jar hit you on the head?'

'No, I licked them all. I licked the tomato and basil one, pesto, alfredo, carbonara...'

'What happened after you finished licking them?'

'The tomato and basil jar was the best.'

To quote Basil Fawlty – 'I can spend the rest of my life having this conversation. Now, please, please, try to understand before one of us dies.'

'I'm glad you liked the tomato and basil jar but what occurred after that?'

'Dad was getting pissed off but I'm sure if he had licked them with me he would've loved it.'

'What did he do?'

'He kept telling me to stop.'

'And did you?'

'Not until I finished the carbonara jar.'

'What did you do then?'

'I looked at the floor and noticed that it was dirty.'

Sam then walks into the kitchen and looks inside the fridge.

'What are you after?' I ask.

'Irish brown bread. I love it, especially with marmalade.'

'Do you want me to toast it for you?'

'I think I should take it to school. They're fantastic at cooking.'

'Sam, it's Sunday, the school's closed.'

'But I can leave the bread, butter and marmalade at the school gates, they'll make it for me tomorrow morning.'

'Sam, let me do it for you. I know what I'm doing.'

'Have you made toast before?'

'Yes, many times.'

'I don't want any dark brown markings on the bread and I don't want those stupid orange bits that they put in the marmalade. They always get stuck in my teeth.'

'I can do that, no problem.' Before he has a chance to change his mind I stick two slices of Irish bread in the toaster and take them out every sixty seconds to ensure there's no 'dark brown markings'. Sam is beside me the whole time watching my every move.

He seems happy enough with the toast's colour when I take it out to butter and then I remove all the orange bits from the marmalade. I've never been so nervous making toast before and feel relieved when he eats it all.

Is he finally beginning to trust me?

I'm tempted to ask whether he liked it but I'm on a high right now and I suspect that he'll burst that bubble with an inappropriate response, so I hold back.

He puts his plate in the kitchen sink and heads upstairs.

'What happened when you noticed the floor was dirty?' I ask him from the bottom of the stairs.

'I ran to the end of the aisle and licked the floor. It needed it.'

'That's good. So how did you hurt your head?'

'Dad got annoyed and pulled my shirt really hard which made me fall over and hit my head.'

Gotcha, Rob. Bang to rights. What a lying bastard, in addition to a cruel and abusive father.

'What did he do then?'

'He was still pissed off but a suit man came and Dad stopped shouting at me.'

'What did the suit man do?'

'We went into a room and they put some cream on my head and told me that the cut was OK. I was pleased that I started to clean the floor but I wish Dad had let me do more.'

'What did your dad say afterwards?'

'He was still a little angry. His face was red but he bought me a McDonalds with extra ketchup and told me not to say how it happened to Mum because she wasn't well. You're not my mum so that's OK.'

'Yes, Sam, it's OK. Now don't forget to brush your teeth. I'll sleep on the sofa again tonight.'

'I've still got twenty-six teeth but I'll count them again when I wake up.'

'One last thing, do you like pasta and the pasta sauce?'

'Nah, it's all shit, but the jars are delicious.'

CHAPTER TWENTY-THREE

After dropping Sam off at school I arrange to meet Maria for a coffee at the same place that I met Jerry yesterday.

'I wonder how long it was before Karen realised she had made a terrible mistake,' Maria tells me.

'Do you mean sleeping with Rob?'

'Yeah. No doubt having Sam kept them together.'

'Karen hoped that having a baby would be the making of Rob and seemingly for a while it was. It didn't last though. She's effectively been a single parent for most of Sam's life.'

'Do you think she wanted to get back together with you when she sent you that message?'

'I don't think so. For all she knew I could've been married.'

'Didn't you say you've got mutual friends? If so, they would've known that you weren't in a relationship and therefore so would she.'

'But I haven't seen those friends for a few years.'

'I think she knew you weren't married. Just look at the situation now. I just find it strange that she's got no one else to turn to while she's recovering. That doesn't seem right to me. She's totally relying on you.'

'I thought that initially but her explanation was plausible. Anyway her sister's going to take over in a week and that's when my stint is well and truly over.'

'So you're just going to walk out of her and Sam's life?'

'That's the plan.'

'I don't believe you. I think you've got close to them and you'll find it hard to break away. Everything has moved on since that eventful London trip.'

'Yes, I've got closer to Karen and Sam but their whole family set up is too stressful for me. Sam is a complete mystery and Rob is just a nasty piece of work. Do I need that in my life? I'll keep in touch but there'll be no more meetings or trips.'

'OK, if you say so. Anyway, how far have you got with the coding?'

'I've written two more programs. I'll email the details later.'

'Thanks so much. That's a massive help. My only worry is that Peter will think I'm some sort of a genius with the speed that I'm delivering this software and will be expecting me to work at this pace all the time.'

'Don't let him know how much we've done. Hold some back. Make him sweat a bit.'

'Yeah, that sounds good. Anyway I hope you have another wonderful night on the sofa and I'll let you know about the meal.'

'I think it'll have to wait until Karen's sister returns and I'm finally relieved of child-minding duties,' I reply.

'When that happens just ring me and I'll order the sausage rolls and the cheese and pineapple sticks,' she says smiling.

We hug each other, then she makes her way back to the office while I wander around London for a few hours before collecting Sam from school.

How my life has changed.

CHAPTER TWENTY-FOUR

'Can we go for a meal, I'm starving?' Sam asks as soon as I pick him up from school.

'OK. But first we'll visit your mum.'

'Nah, let's go now.'

At the risk of upsetting Sam I do what I'm told. I park near St Thomas' hospital and find a Wetherspoons pub nearby.

School's finished for the day so let's go straight to the pub. That's a valid reason why I'll never be a parent.

'So what drink are you having?' I ask Sam.

'Anything, as long as it doesn't have ice.'

'How about a Coke?'

'Yeah, but without that stupid lime thingy they always put in it.'

As we're walking back to our table after collecting our drinks, Sam stops and stares at an elderly man eating his dinner.

'Do you want all of those fries?' He asks the man.

'I sure do buddy.'

'Wow, you're American. I've always wanted to meet one. What's it like in America? Do they still have all those tall buildings?'

'America's great. I'm from New Jersey and they have plenty of tall buildings there.'

'Can I stay at your house?'

'It's probably best you book a hotel.'

'Don't you like Brixton people?'

'I'm sorry, Sam's autistic but thanks for talking to him,' I interrupt.

'That's no problem. I hope you have a great time in the States.'

The American offers to shake Sam's hand but he jumps back.

'He doesn't like anyone touching him,' I say.

'No worries. Enjoy your drink, Sam.'

'When you bump into President Biden can you tell him that I really like his hair.'

The man smiles and nods.

'Sam, you can't ask strangers for their food.'

'Why not?'

'It's their food, not yours.'

'But he's American.'

'What's that got to do with it?'

'They're just fantastic people.'

'Yes, that may be the case but you didn't know he was American when you asked him.'

'He had loads of chips on his plate and he's fat so I thought he'd give some to me but never mind, I still like him.'

Is it the norm for an autistic child to ask other diners for their food? Maybe it is in the autistic world.

Before I have a chance to sit down Sam dashes over to another table, grabs the guy's drink and takes a gulp. Sam obviously doesn't like it and immediately spits it out over the guys shirt.

'What the fuck are you doing?' The guy shouts at Sam.

'That drink was disgusting,' Sam replies.

'Is this your sons' party piece?' The guy asks me.

'No, but he's autistic and doesn't understand why he shouldn't have your drink.'

'Then maybe you shouldn't be bringing him into a pub. Look at my fucking shirt.'

'I apologise. Let me buy you another drink. What is it?'

'Cider, but what about my shirt?'

'Do you want me to pay for dry cleaning?'

'How about the price of a new one? This shirt was expensive and it may be ruined.'

'I really don't think cider will destroy your shirt. Just stick it in the washing machine.'

He doesn't look happy but the guy's an opportunist and I'm not having it.

I buy him another pint of cider and we leave the pub before finishing our drinks.

Well I wouldn't exactly call that pub visit a rousing success.

'Why did you take that guy's drink?' I ask Sam.

'Because it looked lovely and cold. I really like cold drinks.'

'But it wasn't your drink.'

'I know but the man was looking at his mobile phone so I thought he wasn't interested in it.'

'That's not how it works. He doesn't have to guzzle down his beer in ten seconds. He's taking his time. Have you ever done this before?'

'Yeah, every time we go to a pub. Mum always gets pissed off.'

I wonder why?

'You're eleven years old, you shouldn't be drinking alcohol and why did you spit it out over his shirt?'

'It serves him right for having a shit beer. I'm not surprised he wasn't drinking it.'

With this conversation doomed I decide not to pursue it.

How many days until Belinda returns from the States?

CHAPTER TWENTY-FIVE

As we're getting out of the car in the hospital car park my mobile rings – it's Karen.

'Wonderful news, I've just seen the doctor and he said I'm being discharged now. They're arranging a wheelchair for me.'

'That's fantastic. We'll be up in a minute.'

Soon afterwards we enter her room and she's sitting on a chair alongside the bed. She looks the happiest I've seen her since before she was admitted into the hospital.

'Come here, Sam,' she says, lifting her arms towards him.

'You can make my breakfast and dinners now,' he announces, as Karen gently hugs him.

'Maybe, we'll see.'

'So you're free to go?' I ask.

'Yes. They'll have a physiotherapist coming to the house twice a week for the first month to guide me through the exercises and they've given me a bag full of medication, mainly painkillers. I'm just so delighted to be going home. How have you got on with Sam?'

'We just went for a meal and he took a swig of somebody's drink. The guy wasn't happy.'

'That's a normal reaction. I've paid for so many drinks in the last couple of years. I'm sorry, I should've warned you about that.'

'No worries, you've had enough on your plate. I was just a bit surprised.'

'I know I keep saying this but I'm totally indebted to you, Danny. What would I have done without you? I bet you never thought when you answered that Facebook message on Christmas Day that it would lead to this?'

'No I didn't, but I'm glad I was able to help.'

'Can you stay for a few more days, until Belinda returns? I've already spoken to her and she'll come to stay with me when she's back.'

And now the end is near...

'Of course.'

'Is it possible you could homework? It'll really help me out.'

'Yeah, no problem. I anticipated this and I've already cleared it with my boss.'

I hate lying to Karen but the alternative is telling her that I've lost my job because I had to take her son to school. When she's better I'll come clean.

An hour later we're back 'home'. It feels a little strange being back at the house with Karen with so many memories here, good and bad.

With the help of a walking stick and me holding her other arm Karen gingerly lowers herself onto the armchair.

'How do you feel?' I ask.

'Tired but happy. This is the start of my proper recovery.'

'Can I have my chips and steak and kidney pie now?' Sam asks his mother.

'Just give me a little time to rest and I'll make it after that.'

'But you've been resting in your bed for the last three days. Don't you think it's time to get off your arse?'

Karen smiles at her son. She's obviously used to this type of response. One of the autistic behavioural traits that I have since discovered, via the internet, is lack of empathy - Sam has that in abundance.

'Yes, I'll get off my arse shortly and make your dinner. Now in the meantime I want to have a chat with Danny so why don't you watch TV in your bedroom?'

'Is this stranger going back to his Vauxhall house now?' Sam asks, looking at his mother but pointing at me.

'Not yet and he's not a stranger, he's our friend who has been extremely kind to both of us. Didn't you like him looking after you?'

'Sometimes. He never slams doors.'

I'll take any compliment from Sam, even a door slamming one.

Sam goes to his bedroom.

'I'll cook but just tell him you did it. Sam thinks that I'm poisoning him every time I make him something,' I tell her.

'That'll be great. It's just really hard standing up for too long. I hope that changes sooner rather than later. I want to get back to my normal routine.'

'It's going to take time. Don't rush it.'

'I don't deserve your kindness, Danny. Until Christmas Day I thought I'd never see you again. The last day we were together before that was when I told you about Rob and ...'

'How could I forget?'

'Where did you go after you left here that night?'

'I thought about going to my parents but it was too raw. I didn't want to have to tell them what happened. They never did find out.'

'You never told them about Rob?'

'No, I just said we drifted apart. For the first couple of years Mum was desperate for us to get back together. Dad kept a safe distance, affairs of the heart weren't his speciality.'

'They were always so kind to me,' she adds.

'They loved you.'

'I can't believe you never told them. I didn't hear from your parents again. I just thought that was because you told them what happened.'

'No, I didn't. I told them not to contact you.'

'Did they ever find out about Sam?'

'No.'

'You protected me even though I betrayed you.'

'I had a hard enough time dealing with what happened without dragging my parents into it.'

'So where did you go that night?'

'Straight to the Prince of Wales where I had a skinful, trying to get my head around it. At closing time I walked aimlessly and ended up sleeping on a bench in Brockwell park.'

'Oh Danny...'

'I remember a homeless guy gave me a can of cider and it was gratefully received.'

'And where did you go the next day?'

'I stayed at a YMCA hostel for a couple of weeks.'

'What was that like?'

'Interesting. Everyone there seemed to be on drugs. Lots of fights and lots of drinking but I kept myself to myself, going through all my own issues, so whatever was going on around me didn't affect me too much.'

'I didn't know any of this.'

'Why would you? I didn't want to talk to you ever again. In my first conversation with my lawyer I told him that I will not speak to you under any circumstances or even be in the same room as you. I informed him that this had to be a guarantee or I would hire someone else. He did that part of his job very well. I just couldn't believe what you had done to me.'

Karen shakes her head and stares at the carpet.

'I'm sorry, Karen, that's the last thing you want to hear right now.'

'No need to apologise. You're absolutely right. It's obviously been festering inside you all these years.'

'Just forget what I just said, it's old news. I obviously don't hate you now as I wouldn't be here, would I? Now is there a steak and kidney pie in the fridge?'

I manage to cook the meal without Sam suspecting anything.

'The chips and steak and kidney pie were not bad but a bit different. You should've practised it when you were in the hospital because I think you've forgotten how to do it properly. Hopefully it'll be better the next time,' Sam tells his mother.

'OK, thanks for the feedback. Now it's time for bed,' Karen replies.

He looks at her and then heads upstairs without another word.

'I have one last favour to ask of you and it's a biggie. I'm feeling really tired and need to go to bed but I couldn't take my clothes off without help from the nurses at the hospital so can you be a nurse tonight and help me remove my clothes?'

Not many guys would be reluctant if a pretty woman asked them to remove their clothes but I am.

'OK,' I reply. What choice do I have?

I help Karen upstairs and into her bedroom.

I undo the buttons of her shirt and slowly pull her sleeves down. Even though I made this movement very gently Karen winces a couple of times. She's obviously still in a lot of pain despite taking the pain relief medication. Undoing her dress was a little easier but she still gritted her teeth when she had to lift her legs.

So here I am standing in my old bedroom with my semi naked ex-wife in front of me. I immediately turn away from her as I'm guessing she feels as embarrassed as I do right now.

'Shall I get your nightshirt?' I ask.

'Yes, it's in the top drawer.'

I find it and gently lower it over her head. I feel extremely relieved that she's now covered up.

'I'm sorry, Danny for asking you to do that.'

'Don't be silly, I'm here to help you.'

I hold her hand as she gingerly lowers herself onto her bed.

'I feel hopeless.'

'You're going to get better. Just keep taking the medicine and tomorrow you'll start with the exercises. In no time you'll be out and about. Please don't worry. Just shout if you need anything.'

I kiss her forehead and make my way downstairs.

I slump onto the sofa and reflect on what just happened. I haven't really thought too deeply about the logistics of looking after Karen. Will I have to go through this same routine every night and possibly in the morning as well? Do I have to help bathe her? Having slept with Karen for over seven years seeing her with so few clothes on is nothing new to me but the circumstances are a lot different now. As I divorced her over ten years ago I never thought that I'd ever see her again let alone assisting her to undress. However, she is so vulnerable and anxious so how could I not help?

I feel a mixture of emotions about revealing how I was in the time that followed that fateful night with Karen. There's an element of relief that I've finally got it off my chest, but also guilt as the timing of my confession wasn't good. It was the conversation I was hoping to have when we first met up after the Facebook message, but it didn't happen. Karen was very quiet during the meal which could be put down to stress and fatigue but I suspect she was also reflecting on what I said.

CHAPTER TWENTY-SIX

'My aunt will be staying with us on Thursday. Her name's Belinda. She always wears ear rings and white socks. She smiles all the time and has lots of teeth but she doesn't even know how many. When she smiles I try to count them but when Mum speaks to her Belinda closes her mouth. I sometimes tell Mum to stop talking so I can count my aunt's teeth, but she just laughs. I've counted nine so far. I like Belinda because she always gives me money, but if she didn't give me any money then I wouldn't want her coming to my house. Anyway as Mum can't be arsed to take me to school are you going to do it?'

'What time is it?' I ask.

'Three fifty-nine. There's only four hours and forty-one minutes before we leave, so you better get ready.'

I look at Sam but can't muster a response.

'Are you going to be wearing Mum's knickers again?'

'Sam, I never wore your mum's knickers. Why do you keep telling everyone that?'

'Don't you like Mum then?'

'Of course I do, but that doesn't mean I wear her clothes.'

'Do you like dancing?' Sam asks, the master of changing subjects.

'I like watching *Strictly Come Dancing* if that's what you mean?' I reply, although I'm still half asleep. Am I dreaming?

'Do you dance?'

'Only at weddings.'

'What about when you're on the train going into work, or in the pub?'

'I think I'll be arrested if I start dancing on the train.'

'How come I've never seen you on *Strictly*?'

'To be on that show you have to be a bit famous, like a singer, actor or footballer.'

'So if you kick a football in Brockwell Park you'll get on *Strictly*?'

'No, it doesn't work like that. I don't think the TV producer hangs out at Brockwell Park. Anyway, what's with all the questions about my dancing?'

'Because if you could get on *Strictly* you'd be living at the BBC and not in my house.'

'Don't you want me here?'

'No, you're too tall and it hurts my neck whenever I have to look at you.'

It's hard to keep up with Sam sometimes, well most of the time really. Especially when I'm hearing about Belinda's teeth, Karen's knickers, my dancing prowess and my height causing Sam neck problems; and all of this at three-fifty-nine in the morning.

When I was working I was usually up at around seven-thirty and in the Holborn office by nine. However, these recent early morning alarm calls (i.e. Sam) and the conversations that follow have been quite a shock to my system. Yesterday, even though I was half asleep Sam continued to talk about all the different shoe sizes of the kids in his class. Not exactly riveting enough to wake me totally from my slumber but I do remember him telling me that the shoe sizes varied from three to four. He then informed me that the same shoe size range in America is four to five. He wanted his mum to buy him a pair of American shoes on Amazon.com so he could have the largest shoe size in his class.

His logic constantly baffles me but I suppose that's the nature of the beast.

However, within forty-eight hours these early morning discussions will be a thing of the past. Will I miss them? Only time will tell.

Sam now allows me to put the Rice Krispies in a bowl and pour full fat milk over them. This is a major step forward in my relationship with him. He grabs the bowl off me and listens to the crackle of the Rice Krispies for a couple of minutes before eating them. All this time he's grinning and even laughs once. It's the only time he looks happy, as usually all I see is a worried expression.

I check in on Karen but she's fast asleep. I leave a note by her bedside table informing her that I'm taking Sam to school.

'Have you got a lot of friends at school?' I ask, as we leave the house.

'I like Colin because he can't speak.'

'But do you talk to him?'

'No.'

'Why not?'

'There's no point, cos he can't tell me if he likes Popeye or not.'

'Does he know sign language?'

'I think so. Mister Roberts is always talking to him with his hands.'

'Don't you think it'll be nice if you could learn sign language and then you'll be able to understand him better and discover if he likes Popeye?'

'Nah.'

'I know you told me yesterday that you don't want girlfriends but are there any girls at school that you actually like as a friend?'

'Marian is the only girl in my class but she's too fat so I don't talk to her either.'

'Just because she weighs a bit more than you doesn't mean you can't be friends with her. I'm sure she's a lovely girl.'

'I'm not getting involved with fatty people. She'll probably want to eat my Custard Creams and I can't take that risk.'

Sam then dashes over to the post... mailbox and starts licking it. He spends a couple of minutes doing this and covers the whole circumference of it.

A couple of people stop and stare.

'He's autistic, OK. You've seen enough, now jog on,' I tell them rather aggressively.

They look sheepish as if they've been caught doing something wrong, which in my eyes they have. They quickly leave. Sam is of course oblivious to all of this as he carries on with his OCD ritual.

'How did that taste today?' I ask as we continue our journey to school.

'Not bad, about a seven out of ten.'

'Why wasn't it higher than a seven?'

'Too many drops of rain on it.'

That explains everything. I'm glad I asked.

We're greeted at the school gates by Holly, one of Sam's teachers.

'How's your mum, Sam?' Holly asks.

'The hospital has turned her into a lazy zombie and a terrible cook.'

'She's OK but still in a lot of pain. Her movement is limited,' I explain.

'Well please tell her that we all hope she recovers soon and we can't wait to see her.'

'By the way Karen's sister, Belinda, will be doing the school runs from Friday onwards, maybe even on Thursday. I'll let you know.'

'Oh, so we won't be seeing you after that?'

'No.'

'That's a shame isn't it, Sam? Danny's been very kind looking after you for the last week, hasn't he?'

'I wish he was shorter, then his feet won't be sticking out at the end of the sofa when he's sleeping. It looks silly.'

'Why don't you head straight to the classroom and I'll join you in a minute.' Holly tells Sam.

'I thought his father was taking care of him this week?' Holly asks, when Sam is a safe distance away.

'He was, but he got fed up with it after a few hours.'

Holly shakes her head but doesn't respond although it's pretty obvious what she's thinking.

I head back to Karen's and find her in bed reading.

'Are you OK?' I ask.

'Not bad. I was waiting until you returned. I'm not confident moving on my own right now.'

'You were wise not to take any risks. How did you sleep?'

'Not brilliant, as any movement really hurts, but I'm pleased to be back in my own bed.'

'What do you want me to do?' I ask.

'I'm going to have a shower, but if you don't mind staying nearby just in case.'

'No problem, whatever you want.'

I help gather her clothes and hold her arm as she enters the bathroom. I sit on the landing outside the bathroom door and forty minutes later she appears, wearing a loose shirt and shorts.

'Everything OK?'

'Yes, I'm normally in and out of the shower in ten minutes, but I feel a sense of accomplishment that I managed to do everything myself.'

'That's really encouraging. I'll help you down stairs and make breakfast for us.'

'That'll be great, I'll just have…'

'Shredded Wheat?'

'You remembered.'

'Well you did have it virtually every day of our marriage.'

I hold her arm again as we go downstairs. She's moving very slowly with the aid of a walking stick.

'How are you getting on with Sam?' She asks, settling on a kitchen chair.

'Definitely better, although I can't predict what he's going to say or do next.'

'You and me both, but considering you have no parental experience, you've been amazing with him. Not only dealing with a eleven-year-old child but a eleven-year-old with autism. It isn't easy.'

'Thanks for that praise, I'm not sure I deserve it.'

'And I'm so sorry that you had to deal with Rob. He only looked after Sam for a few hours and still couldn't handle it. What a bastard.'

'I think he was using Sam to get back at you. He's so hostile. I don't remember him being like that when we used to hang out together.'

'There were so many support groups for parents of autistic children that I suggested we contact when we were married, but he wasn't interested. It would've helped us, but again his alpha male ego took over. He told me that he isn't wasting his time listening to all that psychobabble claptrap. Instead he used his valuable spare time drinking and screwing around. I don't know why he's so bitter, he's leading the single life that he seems to crave, maybe it's not all it's cracked up to be for him?'

'Yet Sam is oblivious to his father's shortcomings.'

'Sam occasionally asks when his father is going to visit, but most of the time he doesn't mention him so I'm not exactly sure what his feelings are towards him.'

'He did say that he preferred to be with his father in preference to me, but that's understandable.'

'And look what happened when he did spend time with him. A cut head and dumped off at the first opportunity. A normal eleven-year-old boy would've been hurt by that, but Sam didn't seem bothered. At least he didn't say anything to me about it. Anyway we've taken up enough of your time this morning, I'll let you get on with work. Do you normally work in the living-room? If so, I'll rest upstairs. I don't want to disturb you.'

'Karen, there's something I've been meaning to tell you.'

She looks at me with a concerned expression.

'The thing is... I'm unemployed,' I add.

'But at the hospital you said your boss was OK letting you have time to look after Sam. I don't understand.'

'I lied. On the first morning I stayed here I was due to attend an important meeting in Holborn. Clients were coming over from Chicago for it but I took Sam to school at the time of the meeting. It couldn't be re-arranged as the clients were dashing off to Brussels straight afterwards. Anyway, my boss was completely unsympathetic to my situation and told me that he wasn't renewing my contract, which is up for renewal in a couple of weeks. He then informed me I was off the project and told me to get my belongings from the office.'

'But surely he's not allowed to do that?'

'Yes, unfortunately he is. I'm a consultant with a six month contract. There are many reasons why contracts are terminated before their end date but I admit I've never heard of one due to non-attendance of a meeting, no matter how important. I did meet a HR guy but he confirmed that there's nothing I can do.'

'Oh my God, so you've lost your job because of me. I'm so sorry...'

'Don't worry. My boss is an arsehole. I hated working for him. I've already had two employment agency interviews so I'm hopeful of getting something soon. It may be a blessing in disguise.'

'Why didn't you tell me at the hospital?'

'You were so low. I didn't want to add to your problems.'

'I'm mortified.'

'Officially I'm still employed by *FixIT*, well until next Friday anyway, so I've been helping out a colleague who has been lumbered with all my work. I'll be doing some of that today.'

'So meeting me again has been a disaster for you. You spent the last few days living out of a suitcase and caring for my son, the result of an affair that ended our marriage. And to top it off you've lost your job because of helping me. I bet you can't wait to get back to normality. Will I ever see you again when Belinda returns?'

'Of course.'

I fully intend to keep in contact but how involved I'll be in Karen and Sam's life is another matter.

CHAPTER TWENTY-SEVEN
(ALEX)

'Why the fuck did you hand Sam back to that prick? If I'd had known you were going to do that I'd never let you look after him. I did it so you and Mum could spend some time with him.'

'Rob, we know that you did it just to give yourself some respite even though you only spent two or three hours with Sam. Not once did you indicate that you wanted to take him back. You obviously got fed up and didn't hesitate to offload him so please don't give me that crap that you did it for us, OK?'

'I'm his father.'

'Well you had your chance to be a parent and blew it. Remind me again how Sam got that mark on his head?'

'We've already been through this. He fell over running too fast down the aisle at Sainsbury's.'

'We both know that's not the whole story, don't we?'

'Are you saying I deliberately hurt my son?'

'I'm saying that you're hiding something. I can always tell when you're not telling me the truth. I've known since you were a boy when you stole from Mummy's purse and pleaded your innocence but then we found the missing coins in your bedroom. You have that same dishonest look on your face now as you did then. I'm not going to grill you on what actually happened but please don't pretend to be the dutiful father because you're not and I doubt you ever will be. As soon as Sam was diagnosed as autistic you withdrew from him. What sort of a man does that? I'll tell you, a fucking piece of shit. You left Karen to bring up Sam on her own while you fooled around with women. Don't think we didn't know that.'

'Why don't you tell me what you really think?' Rob says sarcastically.

'Your mum and I have always tried to do our best for you. When you failed all your exams and couldn't get a job who took you on? Me of course. And the only person who helped you with your school work was Danny and how did you repay him? By sleeping with his wife. Karen is home now and looking after Sam so good luck in trying to get to see him because she's going to make it more difficult than ever after you hijacked your son and who could blame her? At a guess you're probably not too prompt at paying child support, if at all? But all of this could be irrelevant because I honestly don't think you care about your son. Correct me if I'm wrong.'

Rob looks at me in disgust and storms out of the house without another word.

As hard as it was to tell my son some home truths it's been something I've wanted to do for a long time but I probably wouldn't have if Nora had been in the house as it would have upset her too much.

My only concern is how he'll react. Danny gave me his mobile number so I'll ring him to warn him that he may well get a visit from my son.

CHAPTER TWENTY-EIGHT

I'm getting increasingly concerned. Although it's only a couple of days since I visited the second employment agency I haven't heard back from them but the reality is that this whole process takes time – time to arrange an interview, then attending the interview and hopefully getting called back for a second one. However due to my financial constraints I have little time to play with. All my savings went into my house and I've taken a massive loan out for a loft conversion. I may have to cancel the work. The builders won't be best pleased as they've given up other jobs to take this one on. Even if I do cancel it, it will still cost me as they will want payment for the work done and presumably compensation for work lost. So do I cut my losses? I'm unsure what to do next.

Perhaps I should be more aggressive in my job search but I'm busy looking after Karen and Sam. However, Belinda's imminent return will free me up and I'll be able to return home and back to my life.

Karen's house holds so many memories for me. Our first Christmas there was very special. I remember us putting up the Christmas tree the day after Thanksgiving as we've seen done in so many American films. We were so excited about our first Christmas together in the house we only just acquired and gave each other presents on Christmas Eve, sitting beside the Christmas tree, listening to Bing Crosby and Nat King Cole and drinking red wine. On Christmas Day my mum and dad came over and we went to the pub at lunchtime. I can still recall how everyone seemed so happy. Maybe they were all pissed? I remember Mum asking Karen why she decided to marry me and Karen's reply was 'he's kind, caring, handsome and I love him.' Mum stared at me almost in disbelief that the person Karen was describing was her only son.

From time to time I do think back to Karen's words.

Mum rarely paid me a compliment and never held back from telling me what she was thinking. When I was eighteen I decided not to shave for a couple of weeks. She told me I looked pathetic and likened me to an escaped convict. How many escaped convicts had she come across?

But there are also unhappy memories of this house, most notably my last day here as a married man. I had barely seen Karen in the last few months before we split because of my work taking me all over the country. At a rough guess I'd say I was home half a dozen times in a month and when I was back things were strained between us. I was exhausted while Karen wanted to go out all the time as she was stuck at home during the week. However tense it was I never thought the marriage was in trouble or that she could be seeing someone else. On the night I discovered her infidelity I was absolutely livid. I couldn't believe it. I knew we were going through a rough patch but don't all marriages? We were happy for so many years and to find out she was pregnant with Rob's baby was the final straw. There was no going back and I never doubted my decision to leave. I just couldn't get over how she could throw away something that was so amazing for most of our time together. If I'm honest I've never really recovered from it. Since meeting up with Karen again I've thought more and more about that last day together.

But time is a good healer and right now Karen is physically and mentally vulnerable and I'm happy that I've been able to help her.

Karen has just finished her first physio session and she's asleep upstairs. It's obviously taken a lot out of her.

After finishing coding another IT program I email Maria and a few minutes later she rings me.

'Hi ya, what's up?' I ask.

'Peter knows you've been working on those programs.'

'How the hell did that happen?'

'As per your suggestion I handed the programs over piecemeal but there was one of them that had your name as the programmer and was only written last week so he put two and two together.'

'Oh God, I do that out of habit. I'm really sorry.'

'Anyway he grilled me about it this morning and I had to confess that you were helping me.'

'What was his reaction?'

'He was really pissed off that we went behind his back but legally you're still employed with us so I'm not sure if there's anything he can do about it. Instead he should be thanking you for continuing to work even though unofficially he's given you the sack. You're still being paid until next week, aren't you?'

'Yes.'

'He told me that he needed more time to consider my role in this, so I'm meeting him tomorrow morning.'

'I don't understand that bloke at all. We're going to meet all the deadlines even if I down tools right now, so what's his problem?'

'It's his ego. It's his way or the highway. I'm worried that he's going to let me go as well.'

'How long have you got left on your contract?'

'Two months, but that doesn't matter to him.'

'I can't imagine he'll terminate your contract at this crucial stage of the project.'

'I'm not so sure. Anyway have you heard any more from the agencies?'

'No but I suppose it's early days. So that's it now is it? My work here is done. I might as well stop by the office to drop off my laptop and pick up my stuff, but not when Peter's there.'

'I'll let you know when he's not around. Wish me luck for tomorrow.'

'I'm so sorry that my mistake has put you in this position.'

'No need to apologise, you've gone over and above in helping me and I really appreciate it.'

'Please don't worry. I don't think he'll be that stupid again.'

Despite my encouraging words I fear for Maria's future at *FixIT*. Peter is vindictive and not happy at being deceived, albeit for the benefit of the project he cares so much about. He's also a control freak and that's what worries me. I also feel bad that my mistake has put Maria's job at risk.

Earlier Alex called saying that Rob was really angry that I had taken Sam back. He wanted to warn me that

I would likely get a visit from him. To reduce the chance of meeting Rob I leave a bit earlier to collect Sam. Maybe Rob will be there and if so I'll have to stand my ground this time but I feel nervous at the prospect of a confrontation, especially in front of any teachers or parents. However when I arrive at the school gates there's no sign of Rob and I don't have to wait long until Sam appears.

'Can we go fishing now?' He asks.

'In Brixton? I didn't know that you were interested in fishing.'

'I watch a lot of fishing videos on YouTube. They're fantastic.'

Not my cup of tea but each to their own.

'I love the way the fish wiggles when it comes of the water, it makes me laugh. Is the fish having a dance cos it's pleased to be out of the water?'

'No, the opposite, it's scared.'

'I want to see them dance so can we go fishing?'

'Speak to your mum about it,' I reply, passing the buck.

'Can I buy a fishing rod at the newsagents?'

'No, they don't sell them but I can look on the internet.'

'Nah, if they don't sell them at the newsagents then I don't want one.'

That interest was short lived.

As we're walking away Sam spots his school friend Colin, with a woman, who I assume is his mother.

'Hi, Colin, this is the tall man who picks me up every day. He loves Roger Moore but can't be arsed taking me fishing,' Sam tells his class mate.

Colin replies making hand signals and I remember Sam telling me that he is non-verbal.

'Hi, I'm Jennifer, Colin's mum. He just said that fishing is only for unexciting men who like sitting on their bottoms all day long.'

'I couldn't agree more. My name's Danny, I'm a friend of Sam's mother.'

'Apparently Sam asked one of the teachers if he could learn sign language to find out who Colin's favourite James Bond is and if he liked Popeye. That was very sweet of you, Sam and I can tell you that Colin's favourite James Bond is Daniel Craig and yes, he loves Popeye.'

'OK, I don't need to learn the sign thingy now,' Sam replies, as he walks away.

'That's autism for you, lovely to meet you. I better catch up with Sam,' I say and follow him.

Jennifer nods and smiles.

'I think you should still learn the sign language. Colin will be really happy if you do,' I tell Sam.

'Nah, can't be bothered. I know everything about him.'

I'm sure there's more to know about Colin other than the fact he likes Daniel Craig and Popeye but I'm pleased that Sam actually asked about doing the sign language based on my suggestion. That makes me feel good.

As I drive away I stop at the approach to a zebra crossing outside the school. There's a couple of cars in front of me but I see Rob walking across the road at a pace. He hasn't seen us and luckily Sam hasn't noticed his father.

So it seems I was right to arrive earlier. But why is he here? Karen's home now, so it's back to the same set up as before, with Karen looking after Sam, albeit with my help and later Belinda's. It's somewhat disturbing seeing Rob and his aggressive body language.

I was thinking of taking Sam to McDonalds but decide to head back to Karen's instead just in case Rob makes an appearance.

CHAPTER TWENTY-NINE

'Did Rob ever want to get back with you?' I ask Karen, as we're having a cup of tea.

'Initially he kept calling me screaming obscenities. Most days he rather affectionately called me a whore but then it all quietened down and the few times he came to collect Sam he did ask if we could get back together. I almost felt sorry for him at one point but again it was probably his alpha male ego that was offended. I always assumed he had lost interest in me but he soon went back to verbally abusing me. I got used to it.'

'Still, really unpleasant though.'

'I could've done without it, but concentrating on bringing up Sam virtually took up all my time.'

'Was Sam affected?'

'Overall he was OK. He did ask a few times why his father didn't live with us anymore.'

'And what did you say?'

'I told him that he wanted to sleep on his own so that's why he moved out. Unfortunately due to Sam's innocence, not only because he's eleven years old, but more to do with his autism, you can tell him anything. He's very vulnerable.'

'That's worrying for you.'

'Yes it is and that's not going to change too much.'

'Have you dated anyone else since?'

'Yeah, a couple of times but even if we got past the first few dates and they met Sam it always ended abruptly.'

'Why's that?'

'Just Sam being Sam. Nothing more. He told one guy that his face looked like a confused goat.'

'Surely he must've seen the funny side of that?'

'No, he certainly didn't. I know that a single mother can be a turn-off for some guys. It'll have to be a special person to take on Sam but I get that. After a while I knew it was a waste of time so I gave up dating.'

'Why do you think Rob was at the school today?' I ask, after a pause.

'I don't know what's going through his mind. You being back here has obviously pissed him off. He can always see Sam but it has to be done in compliance with the divorce agreement.'

'Which is?'

'He can take Sam out twice a week but has to bring him home. The situation at the hospital was unknown territory. As I was incapacitated who legally is the next in line to look after Sam? I've never thought about it, least of all had anything agreed and Rob took advantage of that. I should've contacted my lawyer when Rob took Sam without consulting me but I was in so much pain and taking lots of medication; I just wasn't functioning.'

'Don't blame yourself, it's all down to Rob.'

Sam enters the living-room.

'Mum, I haven't seen my ants for a few months even when I bring them my Starbursts,' he says.

'It's too cold for the ants to come out right now. You'll have to wait until the weather gets better,' Karen replies.

'What date is that?'

'I dunno, maybe in May?'

'OK, I'll wait til then.'

'I'm going to pop out to the garden to check if they're hanging about.'

'Do you mind if I join you?' I ask.

Sam looks at me but doesn't answer my question.

'The ants' lives are really boring. They just lounge around until I give them the Starbursts and then they go crazy. They really look like they're laughing and joking with each other,' he tells me as I follow him out to the garden.

I'll take your word on that one.

'I used to give them a bath by pouring water over them but then Mum told me that I probably killed them. I thought they weren't moving cos they were so relaxed after their bath. But I was so upset that I killed them so I don't give them a bath anymore.'

'That's probably wise,' I say.

'I just don't want them to starve and loose weight. I want them to be fit and healthy.'

I don't ever recall seeing an overweight ant but then again I'm not an ant expert.

'I don't like singers,' Sam announces suddenly. Once again he's the master of changing the subject.

'Why's that?'

'They're show-offs.'

I nod. He's got a point.

'And they're always smiling and making a racket.'

'Would you like to play an instrument?' I ask.

'Nah, all those guitars and pianos I see all the time on the TV are just crap.'

'Is there a singer that you like?'

'No. Mum only plays her CDs when she thinks I'm asleep but I wait until she goes to bed and then I put the CD in the rubbish bin. I cover it up with Starburst wrappers so she doesn't see it. Last week I put a Bruce Springsteen CD in the bin. He was giving me a headache with his shouting. What a silly man. I couldn't sleep until I got rid of Springsteen and his noise.'

As I'm a Springsteen fan I feel it's best I don't comment.

After the ants and Springsteen revelations we head back into the house.

'No ants?' Karen asks.

'Nah, I'm going to do a search on the internet to find the exact date when the ants will return to Brixton,' Sam replies.

'OK, that's good. Now give me a kiss and get ready for bed.'

Sam kisses his mother on the forehead and walks past me.

'Aren't you going to say goodnight to Danny?'

Sam turns and stares at me for a few seconds before departing.

'I still haven't won him over, have I?' I say, disheartened.

'I disagree. Having an ant conversation with him is a step forward.'

'You think so?'

'Yes. He was so wary of you at the beginning but now he's definitely warming to you. I mean when was the last time he referred to you as a stranger?'

'Not for a while. I suppose he does talk to me a bit more. By the way have you got any Bruce Springsteen CDs?'

'Why do you ask?'

'Because every time you play a CD when you think Sam's asleep he waits until you've gone to bed and sneaks downstairs and promptly throws them in the bin. He's very careful in covering his tracks.'

'Wow, I don't believe it. I thought I was going senile, losing all those CDs. I didn't suspect a thing.'

'Rest assured you're not going senile. Anyway can you have a drink with your medication?'

'Funny enough I did ask that at the hospital and they said yes, in moderation.'

'Do you fancy a glass of wine? I bought a bottle earlier.'

'Yes, that'll be nice, for medicinal purposes only of course.'

'Naturally.'

I pour Karen a glass of wine and fetch a beer for myself.

'Well here's to a speedy recovery,' I say, as we click glasses.

'So what sort of future do you envisage for Sam?' I ask.

Karen rolls her head back and closes her eyes.

'I'm sorry, we can talk about something else,' I quickly add.

'No need to apologise, it's just a subject matter that I tend to avoid but at a rough guess I'd say that Sam will be in an autistic school until his late teens. Will he be able to take any GCSE's? I've no idea at this stage, but it's extremely unlikely that he'll go to college or university. Will he get a job? Again way too early to say but I do know that he will need special care for the rest of his life.'

'Do you think he'll be living with you indefinitely?'

'Yes, I hope so, unless he becomes unmanageable and then he'll have to go to a special needs care home. One of the parents whose child is in Sam's class also has an older autistic son and he's in a care home, simply because she couldn't cope. I really can't predict what the future holds.'

'All quite sobering.'

'Indeed,' she replies, taking a rather large gulp of her wine.

'Anyway, do you mind if we talk about something else?' She adds after a short pause.

'Of course, I didn't mean to upset you.'

'You haven't. Sam's future is always on my mind. Am I different to most other mothers? No, not really, but Sam's future will be a lot different to most. A while ago I went to Chessington World of Adventures with Sam and while waiting in the queues for the rides I heard numerous conversations amongst parents of normal children. A lot were moaning about how hard it is bringing up kids and I thought if you had to spend a week with Sam you'll realise how good you've got it. Sam's so different from any child I've ever met. His future is going to take a different path from most. The children without special needs will probably go off to university, get a job, get married and lead an independent life. I don't think any of that applies to Sam. I shouldn't compare my situation with other parents but sometimes I can't help it.'

'I can definitely see how difficult it is for you. It must've been heartbreaking when you got Sam's autism diagnosis.'

'It took us nearly six months to see an autism specialist at Guys hospital. Our local doctor was sure Sam was autistic but we needed the official diagnosis in order to proceed with his appropriate education needs.'

'And that's when he was four?'

'Yes, that's right.'

'Was he ever in a normal pre-school?'

'Yes and that was part of the problem. Even at that age he was so far behind his peers on so many levels. He didn't make any friends there and was bullied.'

'Oh God, what happened?'

'Nothing physical, teasing mostly. They kept calling him thick. Kids can be so cruel, even four-year-olds.'

'So what did you do?'

'I quit my job and looked after him for nearly a year.'

'How did you manage financially?'

'I received benefits plus Rob was working but it wasn't easy being with him 24/7. It took its toll.'

'Was Rob any help?'

'Financially more than anything else.'

'It seems a drastic step to take Sam out of school. Did the school do anything to rectify the situation?'

'They went through the motions of contacting the parents of the offending kids and it quietened down for short periods but soon picked up again. We went through several of these cycles before I decided to take him out permanently. It was so distressing even though most of it went over Sam's head.'

'Wow, you've really been through it, haven't you?'

'I suppose, but I know other parents who went through a similar situation. I befriended a couple of the mothers and that was a comfort as we shared our problems.'

'So getting back to your visit to Guys, how did they confirm that Sam was autistic?'

'They gave him standard tests like fitting a square object into a square hole etc but he kept trying to force it into a circle or rectangle hole and got really angry when it didn't fit. They tried to engage him in conversation but his responses were totally out of context. He never once made eye contact with the specialist, he just stared at the floor the whole time. The diagnosis was a no-brainer but things started to move once we got the official word and got Sam into an autistic school for five-year-olds and upwards shortly afterwards.'

'What was Rob's reaction?'

'He dismissed it. He said that Sam was just a bit slower than his peers and that he'd catch up. It was only a short time later that he realised that he was wrong and then Sam lost him as a father. It was a slow process but to me it was all very evident.'

'All of this makes my own problems these last few years pale into insignificance.'

'We all have problems and in your own situation they may seem insurmountable. Remember you went through a divorce after your wife had an affair. Very few people have problem-free lives.'

'All the same, you've been through more than most. Another glass?'

'I'll pass, thanks. I'm feeling tired. I think I'll go to bed.'

'OK, do you want any help?'

'I think I can manage. I'll give you a shout if I can't.'

'OK, goodnight.'

Karen smiles and slowly makes her way upstairs.

I settle down to my penultimate night on the sofa. My back will be extremely grateful when I return to my own bed but how will I feel about leaving Karen and Sam? I really don't know but I'll soon find out.

CHAPTER THIRTY (ROB)

That bastard beat me to it. All I wanted to do was pick up my son and take him for an ice-cream before dropping him back at his mothers' but flavour of the month, Danny, anticipated my intentions and got there extra early.

My dad obviously told both Karen and Danny about our argument.

Of course I should contact Karen before taking Sam anywhere but I'm fed up asking her permission when it's anything to do with my son. Yet she gives Mister Goody Two-Shoes the right to take Sam back and forth to school at will. How is that fair?

I always thought that Danny was a bit of a wimp. After all what did he do when he discovered we were having an affair? He buggered off without even confronting me. But after our recent exchanges I think he's developed a backbone. I suppose I shouldn't underestimate him.

He's only been back on the scene a matter of weeks and yet it looks like he's fully adopted the father role. He must take great delight that he's back with my ex-wife and building a relationship with my son.

Sam told me that he even took him to that ridiculously expensive Gordon Simmonds restaurant in Chelsea.

Is he attempting to buy my sons affections? Is all of this a plan to get some sort of a revenge on me?

I always have to doff my cap to my ex-wife these days. There's no question that she now has the upper hand in our relationship when for most of our marriage it was me who called the shots.

So what can I do about this situation? On the surface nothing, but I'll think of a way to let them know that I'm no pushover.

CHAPTER THIRTY-ONE

'I'm going to tell Mum to get a bigger sofa. Seeing your feet hanging out in the morning is disgusting,' Sam informs me.

I glance at my mobile and see that it's four-forty. Sam is a very early riser and it's obvious he wants other members of the household to be as well.

It feels like groundhog day.

'I wouldn't bother, Sam, because tonight's my last night here. Belinda's taking over from tomorrow, remember?'

'Yes, and she better bring me lots of cash.'

Who was it that said money can't buy you love?

'Will she be speaking with an American accent and asking everyone if they're having a nice day?'

'I doubt it, she's only been over there for two weeks.'

Like Karen, Belinda is a nice person. The sisters were always very close and still are. Belinda is darker and taller than Karen, but with the same model looks as her sister. I recall that she was rarely in a relationship for longer than a few months and that was always a mystery to me. Perhaps she was just happy being on her own without the hassle that comes with a relationship. She was always nice to me and I wonder how she took it when Karen and I split up? After all it was Karen's fault that our marriage ended. However at the end of the day blood is thicker than water. It'll be nice to catch up with her tomorrow but I'm a little nervous as it might be awkward after all these years.

'Is your mum up?' I ask Sam.

'Don't know but I'm not going into her bedroom in case she's snoring. That's gross. It gives me a headache.'

'What else gives you a headache?'

'Car horns, Mum cutting my fingernails, balloons popping, the clapping at that Ant and Dec show, squeaky shoes, music and especially Bruce Springsteen.'

That's quite an eclectic list.

'I see you've had your bath already,' I say.

'I always take my bath before five because I like to lay in the bathtub when it's very quiet. After five I can hear the Brixton trains and I can't concentrate on washing myself properly.'

Will I ever understand Sam's logic? He is my only exposure to autism but do other autistic eleven-year-olds think along the same lines? I've no idea.

Listening to Karen talking about Sam's future prospects yesterday was difficult. I felt for her as she got quite emotional talking about it to me. Because of his special needs she will be looking after Sam for the rest of her life whether he's living with her or in a care home. She will always have to make decisions on his behalf. That's the ultimate commitment.

To think that the years after our divorce I was bitter and angry towards her for the way she ended our marriage but at the same time she was busy dealing with a new born and then later the autistic diagnosis and the problems that brought. The more I've got to know Sam the more I realise how difficult Karen's life has been.

How do I feel now it's my last day at Karen's? It's been such a whirlwind of emotions this past week that it's hard to take it all in. In the first couple of days after Karen's accident I was so stressed out I couldn't sleep. I didn't have a clue about how to cope with Sam, he didn't come with an instruction manual. On a more positive note I've got into a bit of a routine with Sam in the last few days, taking him to and from school etc and there have been less hurtful comments directed at me although I know that they are not meant to be cruel, he just says what he's thinking and simply doesn't know that it could cause offence. We've even engaged in some half sensible conversations. I've grown to like him. I hope that he isn't so wary of me as he was initially.

But can I just cut off my relationship with Karen after everything we've just been through? I don't know. Maybe it'll all be clearer once I've been away for a while.

'Well aren't you going to get your floppy feet up to the shower? Otherwise we're going to be late,' Sam tells me.

'It's four hours to go before we leave, we're not going to be late.'

'But you walk so slow, even with those big feet.'

I can't help but smile but he's looking very serious. Humour really isn't Sam's thing.

I make my way up to the bathroom before Sam has a panic attack.

CHAPTER THIRTY-TWO

A couple of hours later the three of us are sitting around the kitchen table. Sam with his Rice Krispies, Karen eating her beloved Shredded Wheat and me tucking into my Corn Flakes. If anyone was looking in from the outside we'd be the image of a proper family but the truth is very different.

'So today's your last school run, that must be a relief for you?' Karen asks.

'Not at all. It was weird at the beginning, especially when Sam told the teacher that I was a stranger and I left my ID back here; that took some explaining. But I soon got the hang of it and even got chatting to some of the parents.'

'Did you get any phone numbers from any of the single mums?'

'No, but they did ask a lot of questions about our break up once they found out who I was but don't worry I didn't divulge too much. However, that didn't stop them pressurising me for more detail.'

'Yeah, us mums love a bit of gossip.'

'Most of the ladies that I spoke to were single mothers and a couple of them even told me the circumstances behind their separation or divorce. I was surprised how much they told me considering I barely knew them.'

'They're lonely and just need someone to talk to. Life's been hard for them.'

'Are you lonely?'

'Yes, I suppose I am. Belinda sleeps over sometimes and we have a wine and movie night but that's about it. My life revolves around Sam. The only person I ask to look after him is Belinda and that's so I can go to the supermarket on my own. It's a lot quicker and easier getting around the store without Sam licking all the products. The other day he licked the peppers and as usual I got some dirty looks from customers so I ended up paying for the peppers. Whatever he licks I usually put in my basket. Solo supermarket visits aside I don't get any respite and I do sometimes crave adult conversation.'

'How do the general public react to him? As you know I was with him when he asked an American man if he could have his chips and stay at his house in New Jersey. The guy seemed OK about it.'

'At least he asked, normally he just helps himself.'

'Really? What happens then?'

'The initial reaction is usually anger and sometimes leads to a confrontation. Even after I clarify things some diners are still pissed off at losing a couple of chips. I mean get a life. I nearly always pay for an extra portion of chips. It does put me off going to restaurants.'

We're talking about Sam as if he's not there but he's sitting alongside us at the kitchen table. I'm sure he's heard our conversation but he hasn't reacted to anything.

'He does stop people in the street and will typically inform them what they're lacking physically. Last month he stopped a guy with a receding hairline and told him he that looked like a peculiar alien and then advised him to buy a Johnny Bravo wig on Amazon,' Karen continues.

'Don't all aliens look a bit peculiar?'

'Hey, don't paint all aliens with the same brush.'

'What was the guys reaction?'

'He was bemused. I told him that Sam was autistic but didn't wait for any response. But what's worse is his OCD habit of licking strangers. It's usually on their back, so if they're wearing a jacket they often don't even notice but sometimes he'll licks their hands which as you can imagine doesn't go down well.'

'Wow, that must be so difficult for you.'

'It is and I totally understand why people get pissed off but I can't stop him doing it. He gets very angry if I stop any OCD behaviour. I can't recall the last time a member of the public took on board his autism when he does that, it's always a negative response.'

'So is there a solution?'

'His OCD is what drives the licking. He has been recommended various drugs but even with the drugs he'll always have it, to a greater or lesser degree. Plus I'm reluctant to give drugs to a eleven-year-old. Autism and OCD are linked and they are both a lifelong condition. It's about managing them both.'

'The more you tell me and the more I experience autism the more I'm amazed how you can keep it together so well. You are incredible.'

'Thanks, I'm not sure I deserve such praise. If you were in the same situation you'd cope. You've proven that already this week.'

'I'd struggle big time. I've had just a few days of it and I'm absolutely shattered, both mentally and physically.'

'Sam, are you ready to go to school?' Karen asks.

'Have you lost interest in me now? Do I have to find someone else to walk me to school every day?' Sam replies.

'Sam. I'm still not able to walk that distance but hopefully in a few weeks I will be. Just be patient with me. And no, I haven't lost interest in you, I will never lose interest in you.'

'If you say so…'

Karen looks at me and shrugs her shoulders. I can tell she's disappointed at Sam's response but she's probably used to that sort of remark.

'Sam, when your mum had the road accident she broke her hip and had to have an operation to make her better. But her hip is still very sore so she can't walk much at the moment. However, she will get better and when she does she'll be walking with you everywhere,' I explain to Sam on our way to school.

'But why did she have to run into the road? That was stupid.'

'She did it to save you, otherwise you would've been hit by a car and you'd be in the same amount of pain that your mother is in right now,' I reply. I left out the part where it could have killed him.

I still don't get why he hasn't grasped the fact that she dashed onto the road to pull him back and not for the fun of being knocked unconscious by a car?

'So she didn't do it to relax in bed afterwards? I thought she just loves to hear her own snoring?'

'No, she did it so you wouldn't get hurt. She was very brave.'

'Oh, OK then.'

I feel elated he's taken on board my explanation and I can't wait to tell Karen. But what I said wasn't much different to what Karen had told him. He's still a mystery to me.

'Who's your favourite teacher?' I ask, but he ignores my question and rushes to the mailbox. I jog behind him just in case he decides to make a detour and he again licks all around the circumference of the mailbox. Karen discourages this but I can't bring myself to stop him doing something he feels compelled to do.

A couple of teenagers laugh at Sam as they walk past.

'This boy has got autism, if you don't know what this is just ask your parents but don't ridicule him, OK?' I shout at them. They both look at me, shrug their shoulders and move on.

Anyone with half a brain cell would realise that something was not quite right with someone who licks a mailbox, so why did they have to deride Sam? No compassion whatsoever. Is this typical of the sort of shit that Sam and Karen have to put up with? I'm glad I stood my ground. I'll defend Sam against anyone.

'Did the licking go well?' I ask after he completes his ritual.

'Yes, the sun made the red paint shine brighter which makes it easier for me.'

I'm fast becoming an expert on the intricacies of mailbox licking. Could I use it as a subject on *Mastermind*?

'Why were those boys laughing at the mailbox? The mailbox isn't funny, it's very serious. It's for posting letters you know.'

'I think one of them was telling the other one a joke and they just happened to be looking at the mailbox,' I lie.

He nods but doesn't respond. Luckily he didn't question why the person telling the joke laughed at the end of it, surely he's heard it before?

'Do you think Aunt Belinda will give me lots of cash every time she walks me to school?'

'No, I don't think so.'

'But whenever she gives me cash I can see there's loads of notes still left in her purse. Is she being greedy?'

'No, she's very generous to you. Do you thank her when she gives you money?'

'Only when Mum tells me I have to. Aunt Belinda's job is to give me cash notes.'

'What do you do with the money?'

'I put it in a box underneath my bed. I want to go to America to see cowboys and everyone eating in those diners.'

'How much have you got?'

'One hundred and eighty-five pounds.'

'Wow, your aunt is really kind to you.'

'But she still has enough cash in her purse to get me on a plane to see the cowboys.'

'Don't worry, you'll see them one day.'

'What date is that?'

'I haven't got an exact date but I'm confident it will happen.'

I hope by saying that I haven't put too much pressure on Karen but once I secure a new job I will do my best to help Karen and Sam go to the States. Sam has been dealt a cruel hand in life so he deserves to fulfil his dream

I drop him off at school and on the way home my mobile rings. It's Maria.

'Hi ya, I didn't hear from you yesterday, did it all go OK?' I ask.

'No, quite the opposite. He's terminating my contract in two weeks' time.'

'What an arsehole. So he's making sure you complete the coding of the remaining programs and then letting you go; unbelievable. Is there anything you can do?'

'No. As you know they can terminate contracts any time they like. It's just a question on how much they will pay you up to. It's an ego thing with him. We both went behind his back and that pissed him off big time.'

'I'm so sorry, Maria. This is all my fault. If only I had attended that first meeting this wouldn't have happened.'

'No need to apologise. Every action you've taken has been done with good intentions, like helping your ex-wife when she was in hospital and continuing to work when your contract was terminated. You've done nothing wrong. As you said it'll be a blessing in disguise as I couldn't stand working for that prick any longer.'

'With your skills you'll find another consulting job pretty quickly, so please don't worry.'

'You know what? I'm going to book a flight to Florida to see a cousin of mine. It'll be a nice break and something to look forward to.'

'Sounds like a great idea. I'm pleased you're adopting a positive approach.'

It was nice of Maria to say it wasn't my fault but the reality is she lost her job because of me. If only I hadn't put my name against that program that I coded she would've got away with it. It was careless but a force of habit. I will recommend her to the employment agencies that I've contacted even though she'll be in direct competition with me. It's the least I can do. By sheer coincidence just before I arrive home the second employment agency ring me.

'I've pulled out all the stops and got you an interview for today,' the chap informs me.

'That's great. Who is it with?'

'An excellent consulting company in the city. I'll email you all the details and they're willing to match your salary requirements.'

'What time?'

'Three o'clock.'

'Can you possibly change it to four or this morning?'

'No can do. It's three or nothing. They're interviewing all the candidates today only and believe me they act fast. If you pass this interview they'll offer you a job asap as they need to fill it urgently.'

'I can't do it. I have something else on at that time.'

'Change it if you can. This is such a good opportunity.'

'I'm sorry, I can't. But I can recommend a colleague of mine. Her name's Maria.'

'OK, give me Maria's number and I'll give her a bell,' he replies. His loyalty to me is short-lived but that's understandable; his potential commission takes priority.

I hope Maria can make the interview as I know that she'll do well. Technically she is excellent and I have no doubt that her personality and professionalism will stand her in good stead. But it's another lost opportunity for me because of Sam. I can't deny it hurts but what choice have I got? I've promised to pick him up from school for the last time. The timing of it was against me once again. Still, from tomorrow onwards I can devote all my efforts to my job search. I hope the employment agency hasn't lost faith in me.

CHAPTER THIRTY-THREE

'Belinda just texted me. She's arriving back this evening and will be able to take Sam to school tomorrow so you don't have to stay tonight. It's your call,' Karen tells me.

'I'll stay just in case she doesn't make it, if that's OK?'

'That's great.'

I had a chance to leave after picking up Sam. Why am I prolonging it? If I did go home and Belinda couldn't make it I'm only a couple of tube stops away. A week ago, on the morning of the accident, I had made my mind up to walk out of Karen's life but now it isn't so easy. Looking after Sam and Karen has changed me. It feels good taking care of other people and I will miss the closeness of a family unit. It has made me realise more than ever how insular my life is. Karen admitted she's lonely and the fact is I am too. I've shut myself off from the outside world for too long and that's not healthy.

'Coffee?' Karen asks.

'Yes, please. So what sort of things do they teach Sam at his school?'

'They cover most of the basic subjects like Maths, English, History etc but at a very simplistic level. Not that your average eleven-year-old can do a Maths degree but you know what I mean.'

'Of course.'

'They also teach him behavioural management which involves a lot of visual reminders like pictures, flip charts, posters etc, which are displayed on all the classrooms so they can visually see what they are doing and what the next task is. They also do a lot of calming strategies as these kids get extremely anxious over the most innocuous of things. They might use a sensory toy for them to play with or go to a special sensory room where the lights will be turned down low and in the room they'll have bubble tubes which apparently has a calming effect. Soft music is another soothing method that works. Autistic children have a hard time transitioning from one place or activity to another, so the teachers will give them advance warning before a transition is about to occur and again they use visual aids for this. Another topic they cover is the individual sensory needs of the child. For example Sam gets really upset if a door is slammed or even when he's touched so the school try to address these behaviours and attempt to make the child accept them to some degree as they could occur at any time in real life. But it's an extremely difficult task for the autistic child to take on board these strategies as you've already witnessed.'

I nod.

'Whenever Sam does any good work in the classroom the teachers always praise him in an over the top manner just to reinforce positive behaviours. For me these behavioural techniques are far more important that the normal subjects as these will help them manage in the real world. The teachers at his school are fantastic, so dedicated. It's a really challenging job but they are all so enthusiastic and loving towards these kids. Teaching normal children is difficult enough but it definitely requires a special personality to get through to autistic children. These teachers never get the recognition they deserve.'

'Have you ever thought about teaching? I think you'd be great at it,' I say.

'No, it's more than enough for me to manage Sam. I would find it too stressful if I had to do that job the whole day.'

'Yeah, I can see that.'

'Anyway, that's enough about me and Sam. How's your job search coming along?'

'Nothing yet but I need to get my CV out there to more employment agencies.'

I won't tell her about the missed interview today. Why make her feel remorseful?

'Are you worried about your job prospects?'

'Yes, I am if I'm totally honest. I need to get a job as soon as possible. I've got a loft conversion that needs doing and my mortgage is high so I can't be unemployed too long.'

She nods and stares at the kitchen floor. I didn't tell her that I turned down an interview to protect her but now I've made her feel guilty by telling her about my job worries.

'I'll have more time to dedicate to it from tomorrow so I'm sure something will crop up soon,' I add, trying to ease her concern.

'Are you just saying that to make me feel better?'

'No, I'm not. I'm qualified in several programming languages which will increase my chances.'

'Losing your job was my fault. I'm so sorry. I think about it all the time.'

'Please don't worry about that. You've got enough on your plate right now. I'll be fine, I promise you.'

Karen smiles.

'Karen, since we've met again you seem to have spent most of your time apologising to me but the fact is looking after Sam has been a wake up call for me and made me realise how easy my life is compared to yours. All I have to think about is getting to the tube on time in the morning and liaising with IT nerds all day long. It's hardly going to get me a nomination for the Nobel Peace Prize. However, what you and all those parents at Sam's school do on a daily basis is worthy of a prize. You keep Sam out of danger every day of his life and you saved his life last week and even then you blamed yourself. I think you're amazing and I'm so glad you messaged me on Christmas Day. So please stop apologising and just get yourself better.'

'Oh, Danny, why did I sleep with that scumbag when I had you? I must've been crazy.'

'Please, don't torment yourself. Out of that you got Sam and that's a blessing.'

'Yes, you're right. Thanks again, Danny, for everything you've done for me in the past week, I'll never be able to repay you.'

'It was my pleasure, but there is one thing you can do for me.'

'Name it.'

'Another cup of coffee?'

'Done.'

As Karen boils the kettle I reflect on what I said to her. My feelings have obviously been festering all this time but I surprised myself at what I was able to tell her and I meant every word. I had misgivings about meeting her but now I have no doubt it was a good decision. What I don't know is where we go from here.

I spend the rest of the day sending my CV off to various employment agencies, feeling better for doing something positive.

CHAPTER THIRTY-FOUR

I head out to collect Sam for the last time. The first few occasions when I picked him up he gave me a 'not you again' retort but lately he willingly comes to me without the commentary. I walk the familiar streets and stop to look at the infamous mailbox. Just what is his fascination with mailboxes? I know that he has a Post Office fixation but it seems more to do with his OCD licking habit. How the hell can the school break this obsessional habit? He clearly can't function without going through these rituals and it makes me realise that I've so much to learn about autism.

As I approach the school I see the parents waiting. Donna, a single mother, comes up to me.

'Is it your last time picking up Sam?'

'News travels fast around here.'

'Nothing much escapes us. Sam will miss you.'

'I'm not sure about that.'

'He told my boy that you don't slam doors and don't stop him licking the mailbox, so that's as good a compliment you're going to get from him.'

'Yes, I suppose it is but I should stop him licking the mailbox to be in line with Karen.'

'I wouldn't worry about that.'

At that moment Sam appears.

'So what do you want to do now?' I ask.

'I want to go to Sainsbury's in Streatham to make sure that the floor is still clean.'

'OK, Sainsbury's in Streatham it is.'

'What do you buy in Sainsbury's?' Sam asks.

'Lots of things actually.'

'Like what?'

'Milk, bread, butter, beer, chicken, apples, oranges…'

'What else?'

'Broccoli, cheese, Corn Flakes, washing up powder. Will that do for now?'

'Over the last two years we've got thirty-seven different foods from the supermarket. I got Mum to create an Excel spreadsheet and on the headings I put the shopping date and listed all the thirty-seven products. Mum prints it for me just before we go to the supermarket and I tick the items off as I go around the store. But we don't get all the thirty-seven bits every time. On our last trip it was only nineteen. Whenever I get bored I look at all of our shopping trips on my spreadsheet. It's amazing.'

I'm sure it's a fascinating read.

'In our last ninety-one visits we've got milk eighty-five times, that's the leader in my supermarket table. Second is bread with seventy-four and third is bottles of water with sixty-nine. Mum loves water. I think it's such a boring drink.'

'Which product is bottom of the table?'

'Peanut butter. I wanted it because Americans love it and I love butter but it made my eyes go watery. It was crap so we only bought it once. I suppose sometimes even Americans make mistakes.'

'Do any of your school friends have supermarket lists?'

'Nah, they couldn't care less about supermarkets. They're all obsessed with that idiot train *Thomas The Tank Engine*. He's thick. They don't have ants as pets either.'

'Apart from *Thomas The Tank Engine* do they have other interests?'

'Peter likes cricket but only when they play in the white kit. He says it's too distracting when they're wearing different coloured kits. Leslie likes walking up hills but gets frightened walking down them. Alan loves playing chess and collecting chess boards, he has seventeen of them now. His mum wants him to play chess on the computer but he just loves the shapes of the chess pieces and the sounds they make when he places them on all of his chess boards. Ron likes going to swimming pools even though he can't swim. But as soon as someone splashes the water he gets out straight away.'

Not all obvious choices but each to their own.

As we enter Sainsbury's Sam heads straight to the pasta jars and starts licking them. As expected he gets strange looks from other shoppers but I manage to grab a packet of wipes and clean each one as he goes through his ritual.

'Hello, Sam, how's your head?' a man in a suit asks.

'I think the bump on my head has made me grow taller.'

'Well that's a good thing,' the man replies, smiling.

'I'm sorry, how do you know Sam?' I ask him.

'My name's Lewis. I'm the manager here. Sam was in here the other day with his father when he got hurt.'

'Was that when he was running down the aisle?'

'I'm sorry, do you mind me asking what's your relationship with Sam?'

'Not at all, I'm Danny, a good friend of Sam's mother. She was recently involved in a car accident so I've been looking after him while she recovers.'

'But Sam was with his father that day.'

'Yes, but Sam's parents are divorced and Rob was only looking after him that afternoon. The reality is he's a mostly absent father.'

'Yes, I've had dealings with him before. Tends to complain a lot.'

'Was Sam's injury the result of anything Rob did?'

'That's not for me to say.'

'OK, I understand but can you just let me know if I've got the wrong end of the stick regarding Rob's involvement in this?'

'Put it this way your suspicions are not unfounded,' he quietly tells me.

So Rob was in some way involved in the 'accident' but I'm assuming there's not enough evidence to pursue the matter. However, Lewis' reluctant response clearly incriminates Rob. Now it's up to Karen whether she wants to get involved or not. They must have CCTV footage but I'm not sure if she'll want the hassle in order to get to the truth. However it will give her some leverage over Rob should she decide to take it further.

Meanwhile Sam has progressed to kneeling down and licking the floor. I give him a few minutes and then tell him to get up, which he does without argument.

'So what do you want to buy in here?' I ask.

'Nothing. I just wanted to lick the pasta jars and clean the floor.'

Doesn't everyone?

'What else would you like to do? As it's my last day I'll do anything you want, within reason.'

'I'd like some cash to put into my cowboy box.'

'How much does Belinda give you?'

'Five or ten pounds but you can give me more if you like.'

I hand Sam a ten pound note. I would like to give him more but I don't want him to put any extra pressure on Belinda. As soon as I hand him the money I wonder should I have consulted with Karen first. It's too late now.

He immediately stuffs the note into his pocket without so much of a thanks. I expected nothing less.

'So what do you want to do now?'

'I want to see my dad.'

'He's working right now so that'll be difficult but you can visit him another time.'

'Sometimes he gets angry when I talk about ants and lick the pasta jars.'

'What does he do when he gets angry?'

'He shouts and swears.'

'What sort of things does he say?'

'He says I'm stupid.'

'How does that make you feel?'

'I get a horrible feeling in my stomach and his shouting gives me a headache. Mum never shouts at me.'

'But he's nice to you as well isn't he?'

I have no idea why I'm trying to paint a gentler picture of Rob.

'Yes, sometimes.'

'So when is he nice to you?'

'When we go to the pub for a meal. While I'm having my chips and steak and kidney pie he'll drink lots of beer. It makes him smile more and he ruffles my hair.'

'You love your father, don't you?'

'I love him better when he drinks beer.'

Sam still wants to see his father despite the angry outbursts he faces. I wonder what emotions he's not revealing about Rob?

'OK, so what now?'

'I want to visit Leslie's house.'

'Who's Leslie?'

'He's in my class and was born on the second of June two thousand and eleven. He likes walking up hills but cries when he has to walk down them.'

'Oh yes, I remember you saying that. Have you been to his house before?'

'No.'

'Where does he live?'

'At number twenty-seven Thorpe Road in Brixton. It's a flat road so he doesn't mind living there.'

'Do you have his phone number? Maybe we should ring before we go.'

'No, I don't have his phone number but it'll be OK. His mother is always smiling and she has nice shoes.'

'OK, if that's what you want.'

Ten minutes later Sam gently knocks on the door of twenty-seven Thorpe Road.

'Hi, guys, what a nice surprise, please come in,' Leslie's mother says.

She's one of the single mums I befriended at the school. Her name is Sue. We walk into the living-room where Leslie is watching an episode of *Tom and Jerry*.

'What are you doing here?' Leslie asks a little aggressively.

'That's no way to greet your guests, Leslie. They've been thoughtful enough to come over to see you,' Sue tells her son.

'Hello, Leslie, how are you?' I ask.

'Who the hell are you?'

'My name's Danny, I'm a friend of Sam's mother.'

'Is he nice or an arsehole?' Leslie asks Sam.

'Half and half.'

'I'm really sorry about that, Danny. Leslie is very routine driven, he doesn't like surprises,' Sue informs me.

'Sorry, I didn't know. Perhaps we should leave.'

'Don't you dare. Give him a few minutes and he'll be fine. Would you both like a drink?'

'I'll have Coke in a can. If you give me a bottle of Coke I'll have to throw it in the garden,' Sam replies.

'We have cans of Cokes. What about you, Danny?'

'Have you got a beer?'

'Yes, no problem.'

A couple of minutes later she returns with our drinks.

'So, Danny, we thought we'd seen the last of you. Are you still returning to your old life?'

'Yes, Karen's sister will be taking Sam to school tomorrow so I'll be back at my house in Vauxhall. I recently lost my job and need to get cracking on my job search.'

I sound as if I'm keen to leave but I'm not.

'Sorry to hear that. What type of job do you do?'

'I work in IT.'

'I suppose the only good thing to come out of it is that you were able to help Karen after the accident.'

'Yes, in that respect it was good timing.'

Although that is true, it was actually good for Karen but bad for me, jobwise.

'Well, best of luck in your job search.'

'Thanks.'

'Mister Danny, what do you think of my ankles?' Leslie asks me as he pulls down his socks.

'They're very good.'

'I do ankle exercises every day. They're my favourite part of my body. What's your favourite part of your body?'

'I don't know...'

'Come on, everyone has a favourite body part.'

'Your eyes are nice,' Sue chips in.

'OK then, I'll go with my eyes.'

'I don't see what's so special about your eyes, but that's your decision,' Leslie tells me.

'Do you have one of those wives?' Leslie asks me.

'No, I don't.'

'My father left my mother on Friday the sixteenth of July two thousand and twenty-one, so she's now a spare wife, you can have her if you want.'

'That's a very kind offer, Leslie, but I'm afraid I'll have to decline.'

'OK, it's your choice.'

'Sorry about that, he's always trying to get me married off,' Sue sheepishly adds.

'No problem. How involved is Leslie's father with his son, if you don't mind me asking?'

'Virtually non-existent. He had a hard time dealing with Leslie's autism. Leslie just seemed to irritate him all the time. As you've already witnessed Leslie has a thing about ankles and he always wanted to talk to his father about it but rather than show any compassion it would just piss his father off. Something as simple as that and it was just one of many things that really bugged him about Leslie. That wasn't the kind man I married. His attitude totally baffled me. How could he not empathise with his sons' predicament? My husband started going out after work with colleagues more and more and then one night he told me that he was moving in with some tart from his office. He packed his bags and left that night. I haven't seen him since and neither has Leslie.'

'I'm so sorry to hear that. It seems like a common situation from my limited experience. Sam's dad is a waste of space and I feel for the boy as he keeps asking to see his father.'

'I've met Rob and he's a prick. Anyway, Danny, I apologise for blurting out all of that shit about my husband. I'm sure that's the last thing you want to hear.'

'Please don't worry about that. After listening to Karen's tales about Rob I totally emphasise with you. I don't know how you manage to hold it all together.'

'I don't want to slag off all fathers of autistic children because I've met so many that are just amazing, but I've never heard of a mother leaving her special needs child. I've no doubt it happens but it's seems extremely rare in comparison.'

'How do you cope, Sue? Does a bottle of whisky get you through the day?' I ask, trying to lighten the mood.

'Not whisky but I'm partial to a glass of wine in the evening and talking of alcohol, let me get you another beer.'

'Thanks.'

As Sue is getting my drink, Leslie approaches me.

'I'm confused,' he says

'Why's that?'

'When you first met Sam you said you prefer margarine to butter and then suddenly you changed your mind. What are you up to?'

'Nothing. Sam convinced me butter tastes nicer so I've been having it ever since.'

'So what did he say that made you change your mind?'

'He was so passionate about butter that I thought that it must be great.'

'So you have no margarine in your house?'

'No.'

'Do you believe him?' Leslie asks Sam.

'I wasn't sure at first but I think he's telling the truth. I've seen him eat butter on his toast and he was smiling afterwards,' Sam replies.

'That's OK then,' Leslie says.

So I presume that's a not guilty verdict in the butter-margarine court case?

'Did you know Sam likes licking things?' I ask Leslie.

'Of course I do. He talks about it all day long.'

'Do you lick anything?'

'No, my tongue isn't strong enough but I think it's great that Sam does. He's keeping London clean. I think the Mayor of London should give him an award.'

Perhaps Freedom of the City or even Freedom of the Licky?

'So apart from banging on and on about how wonderful your eyes are, what else do you like?' Leslie asks me.

'Do you mean what are my favourite things in life?'

'Yeah that's right, you got it.'

'I like going on holidays.'

'Like where?'

'America, Italy...'

'America's amazing. I just love that Joe Biden guy. He cracks me up. His hair is fantastic. I'd love to have hair like that. But the Italians make pizza, don't they?' Sam interrupts.

'Yes, they do.'

'Well then Italy's crap cos I don't like cheese.'

Dismissing a whole country because of cheese – interesting.

'OK, apart from flying off to America and Italy what other bits of your life do you like?' Leslie inquires.

'I like a beer…'

'Are you one of those drunks that lay on the pavement outside Vauxhall park begging for money?'

'No, it hasn't quite got to that stage yet.'

'Do you start dancing when you're drunk?'

'No he doesn't. He only dances at weddings,' Sam adds.

This is the most surreal conversation I think I've ever had. Where the hell is that beer?

'What else?' Leslie persists.

'I like playing tennis.'

'Can you actually hit the ball over the net?'

'Sometimes.'

'How did you get on at Wimbledon last year?'

'I'm not good enough to play at Wimbledon.'

'So you're shit then?'

'I'm not a professional tennis player. I just play for fun.'

'But it isn't fun if you keep losing. So you fly on one of those aeroplanes to America and Italy, even though they put too much cheese on their pizzas in Italy, you're a drunk and shit at tennis. What else do you like?'

This guy is relentless.

'I like going to restaurants.'

'What type of restaurant?'

'My local Italian one, Mario's, is my favourite.'

'Do you have to take tablets for your Italian OCD obsession?'

'No, I don't. I wouldn't call it an obsession, I just like Italian food.'

'Do they put bucket loads of cheese on their pizzas in Mario's?'

'No, they don't.'

'How do you know that? Have you seen them cook their pizzas?'

'I haven't but it doesn't taste like there's too much cheese on them.'

'So you're just guessing?'

'I suppose I am.' At this point I'll agree to anything to end this interrogation.

'What about you, Leslie? What are your favourite things?' I ask to distract him.

'Hills.'

'Yes, Sam told me about that. He said you don't like walking down them.'

'It frightens the shit out of me. I have to grab hold of my mum's hand cos if I slip I'll roll down the hill and probably die. It's risky.'

'If you're so frightened about going down the hill why do you walk up the hill? Maybe if you stop going up hills you won't get so stressed.'

'So you want to stop me doing my favourite thing in the world? Are you an evil bastard?' Leslie asks.

'Yeah, he can be, especially when his feet are sticking out at the end of the sofa,' Sam chips in.

'Is everything OK?' The slowest barmaid in the world asks on her return.

'This man is an evil bastard as he wants to stop me walking up hills,' Leslie tells his mother.

'I'm sorry, I just suggested that if it frightens him so much going down the hill then maybe he shouldn't walk up it,' I try to explain. I've never given a moment's thought about hills, let alone a lengthy discussion about them; until now.

'There he goes again,' Leslie shouts.

'Leslie, I've been telling you the same thing for ages. You shouldn't walk up hills if it causes you so much stress and Danny's not an evil bastard, he's a kind man who doesn't want to see you frightened.'

'So if he's not evil is he actually nice?'

'Yes, he is.'

'Oh, OK then.'

'Here's your beer, Danny, apologies for the delay, my mum rang. I hope Leslie didn't hassle you too much.'

'No, he was fine,' I reply , even though it's not every day I get told that I'm a shit tennis player, a drunk, got Italian OCD issues and to top it off an evil bastard!

'So, Leslie, apart from hills what are your favourite things?'

'Stop being so nosey,' Leslie snaps back.

'Leslie, what did I tell you about being rude?' Sue says firmly.

'But he wants to know everything about my private life.'

'He's just being friendly. Now tell Danny what other things you like.'

'Bees and Amanda Holden.'

'OK, why bees?' I ask.

'Cos of the buzzing sound and they love flowers, but wasps are arseholes. Bees make me feel calm so when summer ends I get anxious.'

'And Amanda Holden?'

'I like blonde hair.'

'Well thanks for sharing that with me, Leslie. I really appreciate it.'

'It's good to see Leslie and Sam getting on so well. Leslie hasn't got many friends,' Sue says.

'Neither has Sam, as far as I know but he was very keen to see Leslie.'

'How are you getting on with Sam?'

'Better, but I must admit I find it really hard to understand Sam's logic.'

'That's the nature of the beast I'm afraid. They are all such complex kids. I don't understand everything Leslie tells me so don't beat yourself up about it. It's a minefield, even for the more experienced of us.'

An hour later Sam and I are getting ready to leave.

'Mister Danny, you're too tall and it's giving Sam a neck-ache looking up at you. What are you going to do about it?'

'I can't change how tall I am.'

'So you're not bothered about Sam's neck?'

'If Sam's neck is hurting he should see a doctor.'

'But it's your problem. Why don't you throw away your shoes and walk around in bare feet; that'll help.'

'I'll think about it.'

'Or better still, just walk on your knees from now on. That will solve your problem.'

I nod and shrug my shoulders. I'm not sure how else I can respond?

'Apologies for dropping in unannounced,' I say to Sue.

'No apology necessary.'

Leslie is so different from Sam but alike in how his thought process is totally out of left field. He's edgier than Sam and was upset when I offered a solution to his hill problem. However, he came round pretty quickly after his mother chatted to him.

I smile as I think about Leslie's suggestion to take my shoes off and walk around on my knees to ease Sam's sore neck.

CHAPTER THIRTY-FIVE

Well my time with Sam is nearly over. I was actually scared at the beginning of our relationship and when Karen messaged me saying she was looking forward to me meeting Sam I almost backed out. When we met at Brixton tube station on that fateful day of the accident and Sam insisted that I go to Tesco's to get my shoes polished I remember thinking that I had made the right decision to end things after our outing as it was all too much to handle. But now my feelings towards Sam has turned three hundred and sixty degrees. For the rest of his life people are going to give him strange looks and ridicule him like those teenagers did when he licked the mailbox. There's now a huge part of me that wants to stick around to protect him. But would mean getting back with Karen even if she wanted to do the same. Getting to know her again has just been surreal. Oddly, I hadn't talked about my marriage for years until I went for a drink with Maria just before Christmas. Of course I thought about Karen from time to time but as the years rolled by it became less and less.

When we met again I wanted some closure on why she had the affair. I wanted to accuse her of ruining my life but that all changed when I found out about Sam. The accident forced a situation where I had to look after both Sam and Karen. It created a bond with Sam after a rocky start and I'm so surprised at how close Karen and I have become. It's pretty much like it was at the beginning of our relationship. We went to Florida for our honeymoon. On the first night we went to a beach bar and I remember so clearly Karen saying 'promise me you'll never leave me,' unfortunately I did but the circumstances behind that were out of my control.

As I walk with Sam I am more confused than ever about my future with both him and Karen and I actually feel very emotional at the thought of leaving them.

'Why did you suddenly decide you wanted to go to Leslie's house?' I ask Sam.

'To keep me out of my boredom.'

'Did you enjoy talking with him?'

'Yes, because he talks so much, which means I don't have to. It's perfect.'

'Leslie's mum is nice, isn't she?'

'Yes and because she smiles so much I was able to count her front teeth. She has fourteen. I didn't see any gaps. So when will I see my dad?'

'You'll need to speak to your mother about that.'

Sam is longing for a father-son relationship, albeit a different one to most, but Rob is apathetic towards his son. As far as I know Karen has not stopped Rob seeing Sam, so the lack of time that they spend together is down to Rob. I really feel for Sam because I had a loving relationship with my father. He was a kind, gentle man with a lovely sense of humour. My mother was harder, prone to depression, but despite their differences they had a happy marriage. Mum was lost after my father passed away.

In the three years between the deaths of my parents I grew close to Mum. I think she needed me and I was always there for her. It baffles me how parents can neglect their children but of course there's always different circumstances behind each family setup.

Take Rob for instance. He was brought up by two of the most loving parents imaginable and had a great role model for a father in Alex, but yet he neglected his own parental responsibilities. Would Rob had been a better father if Sam was not autistic? We'll never know but it's likely he would have shown more interest.

CHAPTER THIRTY-SIX

Just as I'm entering the house my mobile rings. It's Maria.

'Did the employment agency ring you yesterday?' I ask.

'Yeah, but I unfortunately I couldn't make it. Too much on right now.'

'That's a shame.'

'I was desperate to make that interview and was ready to leave when Peter piled more work on me and of course it was work that needed doing right away. Very frustrating.'

'He's so demanding.'

'But thanks for referring me to them. That was very sweet of you.'

'No problem.'

'Anyway that wasn't the reason why I called. I don't understand why but Frank wants to see us both tomorrow morning at ten.'

Frank is Peter's boss.

'That's strange. Did he give you any clue what it's about?'

'None whatsoever. Surely there's nothing more they can do to us, is there?'

'He might give us a grilling about what happened but at this stage I don't care. It'll give me a chance to return my laptop and meet up with you. Fancy going for a coffee afterwards?'

'Yes, that'll be lovely.'

Seeing Maria is something to look forward to after I leave Karen's tomorrow morning. As for Frank, I haven't had too many dealings with him as he's rarely in the office but from what I've heard he's a good guy and dedicated to his job. Hopefully he's just going to thank us for our service and nothing more.

'What prompted the visit to Leslie's?' Karen asks me as I walk into the living-room.

'Don't know. Sam said he was bored.'

'I'm so glad he went. That's a really positive thing. He needs to have more friends. How did you get on with Leslie?' She asks, smiling.

'He's very lively and inquisitive. Absolutely bombarded me with questions about my life.'

'Yeah, that sounds like him. He's a good kid once you get to know him. How was Sue?'

'She was really nice. Told me all about her elusive husband.'

'I always thought that he was a good guy. Seems he just couldn't handle the situation he found himself in.'

'Sound familiar?'

'But was Rob ever a good guy?' Karen asks.

'No comment. Anyway, how are you feeling today?'

'I've been doing all the exercises and they're definitely helping. I feel more mobile and the pain is less. It's a slow process but I'm getting there. Today is the first day I've felt more positive about my recovery.'

'That's great to hear. As it's my last night do you feel up to going out for a meal? My treat.'

'Yes, I'd love to.'

'Your choice of restaurant. What's best for Sam?'

'He's not really keen on Italian food, especially pizzas.'

'Yes, that much I know.'

'What about going to our old haunt?'

'The Prince of Wales?'

'Yeah, they do excellent chips and steak and kidney pie, so Sam will be happy.'

'Done deal. Do you want me to drive?'

'It's only a short walk so I think I can manage it. I'll have my walking stick and you for extra support.'

'I really don't mind driving.'

'My physio's encouraging me to start walking as soon as possible, so this is a good opportunity to put that into practice. Obviously it's too risky for me to walk with Sam on our own just in case he runs onto the road but if you're walking pigeon steps alongside me then I'm up for it.'

'Pigeon steps it is.'

CHAPTER THIRTY-SEVEN

'Come on, Mum, are you taking the piss?' Sam says as we're nearing the pub.

'What did I say about swearing?' Karen replies.

'But you're walking like a shitty tortoise.'

'Sam!'

The reason why Sam is getting irritated is because Karen is moving very slowly. She is holding onto my arm and leaning heavily on her walking stick but as we're nearing our destination I sense she has slightly picked up pace like a marathon runner who can see the finishing line.

The look on Karen's face as we finally reach the pub is priceless. It seems all the anxieties of the last week have disappeared in an instant.

'Well done, how do you feel?' I ask her.

'Relieved. Thanks for helping me.'

'You're welcome, now let's have a drink to celebrate.'

As we enter the pub Sam dashes over to a middle-aged man, grabs his hand and starts licking it.

'What the fuck are you doing?' the man shouts at him.

'Just licking you, that's all. I don't like the taste of your ring though. The next time you come in here don't wear it.'

'Get the fuck away from me,' the man pushes Sam, causing him to fall over.

'Hey, calm down mate,' I say to him as I pick up Sam.

'How can you allow him to do that? It's disgusting.'

'First of all, I apologise. I perfectly understand why you're upset but Sam's autistic and unfortunately his licking habit is part of his condition.'

'Then you should keep a tighter rein on him in public places.'

'Listen, mate, I've apologised, OK? Have you any idea how difficult life is for an autistic child? Of course not, why should you? Perhaps now you have an idea you could show a bit of compassion or is that too much to ask? It really wasn't the crime of the century, was it? And let me tell you if you ever push that boy again you'll regret it. So get a fucking life, yeah?'

The man looks at both Sam and me and storms out of the pub without responding. That's one less arsehole to worry about.

'Maybe we should go...' Karen says as she catches up with us.

'No way, it's time the public understood that not everyone is the same. They should walk a day in your shoes. They're just getting a minute glimpse of what it's like in the autism world but Sam and you are living it every single day. So Sam licked the guy's hand and I know that's not pleasant but he'll survive, there was no physical injury. I've only just been exposed to the world of autism but I'm already pissed off at the lack of understanding and empathy that the general public show. It's just not right and you shouldn't have to put up with that. I apologised and tried to explain the situation but he wasn't interested. You and Sam shouldn't have to restrict your movements because of idiots like him, otherwise they're winning. Maybe I'm overreacting but that's just the way I feel. Now we're going to get a table and enjoy our evening whether Sam approaches anyone else or not.'

To my surprise I see Karen's frown turn into a beaming smile.

'Wow, I'm touched,' she says.

'I care for Sam and when I'm with him if anyone else reacts like that man did then they'll have me to answer to. I just can't stand the total lack of kindness. I find that so distressing. I get it that your average person in the street doesn't know much about autism, I certainly didn't, but when an eleven-year-old boy starts licking your hand you must know something is not quite right. And I'll just repeat again what I said earlier, of course it's a shock when Sam approaches someone in the way he did tonight but just show some empathy when it's explained why he's doing it. Is that too much to ask? Sam is oblivious of the stress that he is causing and I'm getting increasingly frustrated that you and Sam have to face this every day. It really does fuck me off.'

'I couldn't have put it better myself. You're becoming quite the crusader for autism, aren't you?' Karen says still smiling.

'I suppose so.'

'You've shown more compassion to Sam than Rob ever has. As for you young man please don't lick anyone else's hands tonight, do you hear me?'

'But nobody's wearing gloves, so they obviously don't give a toss.'

It's that Sam logic again.

Karen asks for a table that is furthest away from the other diners just in case Sam gets any ideas and after the licking incident the staff are only too keen to oblige.

'This place hasn't changed much has it?' I say, as we settle into our seats.

'No it hasn't, which is a good thing. Lots of memories within these walls,' Karen replies.

'The karaoke night was fun, wasn't it?'

'Yes it was. I'm still amazed that you had the nerve to get up on the stage to sing *My Way*, considering your voice is… shall we say, pathetic?'

'Harsh. I thought it got a good reaction though.'

'In terms of belly laughs, yes. I presume you've never performed live again?'

'No, I retired at the top. Do you remember the last time we were here?' I ask.

'Yes I do. It was a couple of weeks before we split up. We hardly spoke all night.'

'You were really pissed off that I was away so much and I was absolutely knackered from travelling. Not the best basis for a fun night out,' I reply.

'Correct me if I'm wrong but was that the last time we went out socially as a married couple?'

'Yeah, I think you're right. I know my trips away didn't help our strained relationship at that time but do you think that fact that we couldn't have children was also a factor?'

'Without a doubt. I desperately wanted a child and just couldn't believe that it wasn't going to happen,' Karen says.

'How do you think I felt when I was to blame for that? It should've brought us closer together but the opposite happened.'

'Let's not dwell on our negative past. Right now we're getting along just fine. I'm feeling better, so let's celebrate the positives.'

'Do you remember the Batman TV series?' I ask.

'Yes, that was a long time ago.'

'The sixties. I used to love it when Commissioner Gordon shone the bat signal into the sky whenever they needed Batman's help. Well if you have any hassle with the public over Sam just send a Danny signal and I'll come to your rescue and sort them out.'

'I love that idea.'

A quiet moment follows as we both glance around at the familiar surroundings of the pub we used to frequent.

'We never discussed adoption properly did we?' I say.

The conversation is flipping from light hearted recollections to serious issues.

'No. I couldn't face another disappointment so soon after the baby news but given time I think we would've pursued that.'

'Yes I agree, but we never got that time.'

'Are you two having a baby? I don't like that idea, they don't sleep, they get sick and they shit too much,' Sam announces.

Spot on observations.

'No, Sam we're not having a baby, we're just talking about our past when me and Danny were married. Remember I told you that?'

'So which of the married men did you like best, Dad or this guy?' Sam asks, pointing at me.

'Both the same,' Karen replies, giving me a wink.

'Who wore the nicest underpants?'

'They both wore nice underpants,' Karen replies, laughing.

'Why did the big feet guy leave you?'

'We no longer loved each other.'

That's actually not true.

'So it wasn't because of the colour of his underpants or his big feet?'

'No.'

This is the first time that Sam has asked about our marriage in any detail and it's interesting that he's drawing comparisons with Rob, albeit about the quality of our underpants.

The rest of the evening passes without further incident and to be on the safe side we take an Uber back to the house.

'That was a lovely evening, thanks for your company,' Karen tells me as I'm sorting out my sofa bed.

'How are you feeling?' I ask.

'I think the wine killed off any pain I may have had.'

Sam walks into the living-room.

'That steak and kidney pie was OK but that Simmonds geezer cooked a much better one. Will you take me back to Gordon's or will I never see you again?' Sam asks me.

'You'll definitely see me again and yes we'll go back to Gordon's. I'm not sure he'll be there but if not we'll get someone else to cook that pie for you.'

'That's good because all the other food in that restaurant is crap. He only knows how to make steak and kidney pies. He should have just a steak and kidney pie restaurant instead.'

That's somewhat limiting.

'Anyway it's time to go to bed so give me a kiss,' Karen tells Sam. He kisses his mother on the forehead.

'Are you going to say goodnight to Danny? It's his last night here.'

'Do we have to disinfect the sofa after he disappears?'

'No, that's not necessary.'

'OK, then, but don't make a dent on the sofa tonight cos I want to watch *Friends* on it tomorrow,' he tells me before leaving the room.

'Are you going to thank Danny for taking you to and from school?' Karen asks.

'Nah,' he shouts from upstairs.

That's the first time he acknowledged me just before going off to bed, even though he was warning me not to make a dent in the sofa. In my eyes that's progress. Baby steps.

'I'm pleased that you'll be taking Sam out but that restaurant is way too expensive, can't you persuade him to go somewhere more affordable?'

'Afraid not, believe me I've tried but that's OK, he deserves a treat.'

'You have been so kind to my boy. I'll never forget that.'

I nod. I want to say so much more but now is not the right time. I'll wait until the dust settles and not blurt out exactly what I'm feeling right now.

'Karen, if you don't mind I need to get some shuteye. I feel shattered.'

'Of course. Hopefully your back will survive your last night on the sofa. But promise me one thing.'

'What's that?'

'Don't make any dents in the sofa,' she gives me a cheeky smile before making her way slowly upstairs.

I turn off the light and lay in the darkness contemplating my future. Like most recent nights my initial thoughts are dominated with my job status but tonight I'm also wondering if my future includes Karen and Sam.

After a couple of hours tossing and turning I eventually fall asleep.

CHAPTER THIRTY-EIGHT

'Belinda's not here yet,' Sam informs me.

It's dark outside which means I've been woken up at some ungodly hour again. I glance at my mobile and see that it's four forty-nine.

'It's way too early for her to be here, Sam. Why don't you go back to your bedroom and rest?'

'I don't like resting, that's for dopey people.'

'Do you mind if I go back to sleep for a couple more hours?' I plead.

'No, that's impossible. We need to keep a look out for Belinda.'

'Can't you manage that on your own?'

'No because she parks her car on the other side of the street and walks to our house. It's dark outside and I might not see her. It needs the two of us.'

'But your mother said that she won't be coming until around eight. That's over three hours away.'

'She might come earlier, we need to be prepared.'

'But what difference will it make if we spot her or not? Your mother said she's got her own key.'

'Yes, she's got a key and she always uses it.'

'So it's not a problem, she can let herself in.'

'It is a problem cos she closes the door too hard. She doesn't slam it but it's still way too loud. I need to open the door myself. I just can't risk her doing it.'

'Why don't you ask your mother to help out?' I ask in vain.

'There's no way I'm going into that room with her snoring.'

'Oh OK then, I'll have a shower now.'

'Well hurry up, we don't want to miss my aunt,' he shouts.

Three hours and twelve minutes later we both spot Belinda as she approaches the house. During that time there was little conversation between us. I started talking to Sam at the beginning of our vigil but he told me to shut up as he couldn't concentrate. When I started to read my book to pass the time he immediately took it off me telling me that I need to pay attention to the street activity. It wasn't exactly the most stimulating time of my life and I'm so relieved that it's finally come to an end.

Sam rushes to the front door and very quietly opens it.

'How many notes are you going to give me today?' I hear Sam asking his aunt.

'Just wait and see,' she replies.

'Danny, long time no see,' Belinda says as she enters the living-room and immediately engulfs me in a hug. She hasn't changed much since I last saw her. Her long hair shows no signs of grey (hair dye?) and she is still slim.

'I suppose you get that question a lot from Sam?'

'Every visit, without fail.'

'How was America?'

'Amazing. I love New York, such a vibe and energy to it. I've never been to a city like it. I'd love to live there.'

'Good idea. I'll come with you,' Sam chips in.

'And what about your mother?' Belinda asks.

'I'll spend half of the year with you and the other half with her in Brixton. It's easy. What were the cowboys like?'

'I didn't see any in New York.'

'Fuck that, I'm not going there. I'm going to google where the cowboys live in America.'

With that he dashes upstairs.

'Danny, I'm so grateful to you for looking after Sam and Karen. I just can't believe that you're here after everything that happened in the past.'

'I was somewhat surprised to get that facebook message on Christmas Day and I wasn't sure about meeting Karen but now I'm glad I did. Having found out how her life has unfolded I couldn't be angry with her anymore.'

'She's dealt with a lot but it's made her stronger. I wanted to come home immediately when I heard about the accident but I was really surprised when she told me there was no need and that you had things in hand.'

'I admit I struggled at the beginning but it's been an absolute joy being able to help Sam and Karen.'

'So any chance of you two getting back together?'

'Belinda, how lovely to see you,' Karen says as she gingerly walks towards her sister.

That was a fortunate intervention.

'How's the hip?' Belinda asks, as she gently hugs her sister.

217

'It's getting better, slowly.'

'Look, I'm really sorry to dash off but I've got a meeting in a couple of hours and need to pop home to pick up some things.'

'That's a shame. I was looking forward to having a good old catch up. But we'll see you again, won't we?' Belinda asks with a nervous look at Karen.

'Yes, I hope so.'

'Aunt Belinda, can you help me with this cowboy website?' Sam shouts down from his bedroom.

'My presence is required,' Belinda says before leaving.

'Do you want to say goodbye to Sam?' Karen asks me.

'It's OK, he's focusing on cowboys right now, I don't want to disturb him.'

'Well, what can I say, Danny?'

'There's no need to thank me anymore. You've used up a large quota of your lifetime allowance of thank-yous on me.'

'OK, but can I at least say that I'll miss you?'

'You just did.'

We hug and she kisses me tenderly on the cheek. I smile at her, pick up my bags and leave without saying another word.

CHAPTER THIRTY-NINE

There were many times since Karen's accident when I've longed for the day that Belinda returned but now I find myself wondering if I really want to go back to my old life.

I was on the verge of telling Karen that I have feelings for her again but stopped myself. Why? Does she feel the same? She has been so nice to me from the moment we met up but am I mistaking that for something deeper? I think the reason I held back revealing my thoughts to her was because I'm not sure if it's just nostalgia. Am I just revisiting the early days of our relationship or is it something real? My head is spinning just thinking about it. I need to take a break from Karen and Sam.

As I enter my office for the last time I show my pass to the security guard. I'm half expecting him to take it from me but I'm sure Peter is going to relish doing that himself.

I walk through the open plan office and nod to various colleagues. In fairness I've never really been that close to most of them as all they're interested in is IT. It's impossible to find someone here who knows how Chelsea got on at the weekend. The only colleague I've socialised with is Maria who approaches me as I reach my desk.

'Frank wants to see us straight away as he's got another meeting in fifteen minutes,' she tells me.

'No time for small talk then?'

'There'll be plenty of time for that soon enough.'

We make our way to Frank's office.

'Hello, nice to see you both, please sit down,' he says, 'I suppose you're both wondering why I called you in?'

'Yes, it did cross our minds,' I reply, looking at Maria who nods.

'As you know I travel extensively due to my work commitments but in the past couple of weeks I've been attending a number of meetings in London, so I've popped into the office more than usual. However I never once saw you, Danny. I assumed you weren't on holiday as we were in the middle of the *SignalPlus* project and you were the primary analyst on that, so I asked Peter where you were and he told me that he had terminated your contract as you felt under too much pressure and wanted out. This didn't make much sense to me so I discreetly spoke to a couple of your colleagues who told me a completely different story. So, Danny, can you tell me your side of this? I hate to pressurise you but I've got a meeting in a few minutes.'

'OK, I divorced my wife ten years ago because she had an affair with a friend of mine and had his baby.'

'Is this relevant?' Frank interrupts.

'Yes, it is and I'll explain why. My ex-wife, Karen, facebooked me on Christmas Day out of the blue and the next day we met up for the first time in over a decade. She has a eleven-year-old autistic boy called Sam. Later that week we went on a day trip to London and when Sam rushed onto a busy road Karen managed to pull him back but she got hit by a speeding car and broke her hip. Believe it or not I was the only person available to look after Sam. Her ex-husband, his father, is a scumbag. The morning after the accident I was due to attend the meeting with all the Chicago guys but I couldn't make it as I had to take Sam to school. I rang Peter the night before, which was the actual day of the accident, and explained everything but he terminated my contract as soon as I finished talking. I tried to reassure him that Maria was more than capable of handling things at the meeting and that I would pick up the pieces afterwards but he wasn't interested. As I was being paid for a further two weeks and knowing that Maria would be under intense pressure to meet the tight deadlines I decided to help her out by coding a number of programs but putting her name against them all. Unfortunately I left my name on one and Peter knew that I was still working on the project. He decided to terminate Maria's contract, saying that she had deceived him. I hope that explains everything.'

'Within five minutes, I'm impressed. Your account matches exactly with your colleagues. In my opinion you're both very talented and dedicated professionals and I've never heard of anyone continuing to work after they've been sacked regardless of whether they're still being paid or not. Peter made a big mistake and consequently I'm going to terminate his contract as from today. I shouldn't really be telling you this so please be discreet. What he did was not in line with the *FixIT* company values. I really don't know what he was thinking? It was malicious and that type of attitude has no place in *FixIT*. You've both delivered this project under the most extremely difficult and stressful circumstances so I'm going to renew both your contracts for another two years and on top of that you will both receive a pay rise. I can only apologise for the way you've been treated, it's unacceptable. Now do me a favour and take the rest of the day off. Please accept this voucher for that Gordon Simmonds restaurant in Chelsea; the food is excellent. I recommend the pigeon. My apologies for rushing through this but I've got a day full of meetings, starting now. I hope to see you both here tomorrow, is that OK?'

'Thanks so much, Frank, you don't know how much this means to me,' I say.

'Yes, thank you, Frank,' Maria adds.

'You're more than welcome. Enjoy the rest of your day.'

As soon as I leave the meeting room I ring Karen.

'I've got my job back,' I excitedly announce.

'I don't believe it. How the hell did that happen?' She asks.

'I'll explain later but Frank felt it was an unfair dismissal. He's also given me and Maria a two year contract, which I've never had before, and a pay increase. It hasn't sunk in yet.'

'You deserve every bit of good fortune that comes your way. You were punished for helping me out when I need it the most so justice is done. I couldn't be happier for you.'

An hour later I'm with Maria in the local coffee bar.

'Did you see that coming?' Maria asks.

'Absolutely not. I knew that we were both unfairly treated but I've seen so many consultants let go before their contracts came to an end for various reasons and just assumed that's the way the company works.'

'And Peter getting the chop is just the icing on the cake.'

'No sympathy from me. The bastard got what he deserved. I was going to spend the rest of the week contacting as many employment agencies as possible and now I don't have to, it's such a relief.'

'So we're a team again,' Maria says.

'I couldn't be happier. I felt so guilty that my mistake cost you your job.'

'I never blamed you. You were only trying to help me out. Anyway, changing the subject, how do you feel about finally leaving Karen's?'

'To be honest, I really miss them both.'

'But I thought you couldn't wait to get your life back?'

'I've been part of a family again and it has made me realise what I've missed out on. I think I'm in love with Karen, again.'

'You're kidding me?'

'I'm not and I can't believe it myself. My feelings for her have grown with every day.'

'Wow, I'm shocked. What about Sam? Every time we spoke you were so stressed out with him, you couldn't cope.'

'Yeah, I know but bit by bit I got used to his ways and I now feel protective towards him. I've even had a few confrontations with people who took offence at something he said or did. That just fucks me off.'

'OK, so does Karen know this?'

'No, I'm afraid of getting hurt again.'

'But you have to let her know how you feel.'

'I know but I need more time.'

'We have to discuss this further and need something stronger than coffee, so let's go the pub.'

'No argument from me.'

'One for the road?' I ask Maria, a couple of hours later.

'Yeah, why not?'

'Is everything OK? You seem quiet all of a sudden,' I say.

'I have a confession to make.'

'Sounds ominous.'

'I'm pleased you're hoping to get back with Karen and got close to Sam but these last few weeks I've been getting close to you and I was beginning to think that we might have some sort of a future together, that is outside of work.'

'Oh, Maria…'

'No, it's OK. It's not a problem as it's been nipped in the bud before it had a chance to develop. It's probably for the best as we're going to be working together. I just have to continue my search for that decent guy.'

'I know that we were getting closer but I if I'm honest I never thought about taking it further. Maybe it could've done if I hadn't met Karen again, who knows? I'm sorry if I misled you in any way, that wasn't my intention.'

'Don't be silly, you didn't mislead me. It was just a bit of flirtation. I probably wouldn't have mentioned this to you if it wasn't for all the wine I've drunk but it's done now and I hope it won't make our relationship awkward?'

'It definitely won't. I appreciate you telling me and I'm certain that you will find that guy.'

'You know what I'm going to put my name down on an online dating agency website as soon as I get home. It's been something I've been meaning to do for a while. What have I got to lose?'

'Sounds like a great idea.'

We clink glasses and swiftly move on to gloat about Peter's sacking.

I arrive home early evening. Despite consuming a fair amount of alcohol I don't feel drunk. I think this is because it was spread across the whole afternoon. I was surprised at Maria's confession, given my declaration of love for Karen, but maybe she felt better for being honest with me. I had no idea she felt that way and I feel a bit stupid that I didn't pick up on it. Although she hasn't had too much luck with relationships I'm sure she'll find someone who will love for who she is – a kind and caring person.

I'm still amazed that I've got my job back. I just didn't expect that. And Peter losing his job was another shock but he's only got himself to blame.

I flop onto my bed – another moment I've been dreaming about.

I left Karen quite abruptly this morning, partly due to the need to get into the office but I also wanted to cut short our conversation. Even when I told Karen my good news I kept it brief. I didn't want to let my guard down, which normally comes as second nature to me, being an Englishman and all that, but this morning I struggled.

Just before I doze off I think about Sam. Did Belinda have any problems with the school runs? Did she shut the door too loudly? Is he happy that he watched *Friends* without a dent in the sofa? Is his neck any better now that I'm not around? Did he think of me at all today?

Will I miss our four-forty-nine am chats?

Absolutely.

CHAPTER FORTY (ROB)

'What do you want?' Karen abruptly asks me.

'Is that anyway to greet the father of your child?'

'You mean the father that took Sam without my permission?'

'How could I? You were having an operation and drugged up to the eyeballs.'

'You took advantage of the situation and another thing, how did Sam get that cut on his head?'

'He fell over running in Sainsbury's. We've been through this.'

'That's not true.'

'What are you talking about? Are you still on medication?'

'Danny found out what actually happened.'

'Don't trust anything he says. He's got it in for me.'

'Why do you hate Danny so much? It doesn't make any sense.'

'That arrogant shit feels superior to me and that goes back to our school days.'

'You mean when he helped you with your school work? Anyway I've had enough of listening to your shit, what do you want?'

'Can I pick up Sam this afternoon? I'd like to take him for an ice cream or maybe a McDonalds.'

'No. You're too unstable right now. I don't trust you.'

'So you're denying me time with my son?'

'Yep, I'm impressed you understood that.'

'So if I tell Sam that you stopped me from taking him out do you think he'll be happy about that?'

'That's the sort of thing you would say to him to try and discredit me. No matter how much of an arsehole I think you are I never slag you off in front of Sam but of course you never think like that. Say what you like if it makes you feel better but rest assured you're not taking him out this afternoon.'

'My lawyer might have something to say about that!'

'Oh God, the lawyer threat yet again. Go ahead, fill your boots but let me repeat this once again and try to remember it this time – you always need my permission to see Sam. Browse through your divorce agreement again, it's a wonderful read, I thoroughly recommend it. Anyway this conversation's finished.'

Karen hangs up.

What a bitch. She's ruining my life and I can't take it much more.

I know I haven't been a good father but when Sam is banging on about bullshit it does my head in. I've got little patience for him but I know that he can't help it so I should be more understanding. I genuinely want to take him out for a treat after school but Karen has put the brakes on that.

Danny is determined to build a case against me about Sam's injury. What a bastard!

I shouldn't have been so aggressive with Karen as that didn't help my cause but that wasn't my original intention, it's just she really winds me up. Like her lovesick puppy Danny, she's got a patronizing attitude towards me and I've had enough. I am going to collect Sam this afternoon and I don't give a fuck about the consequences.

CHAPTER FORTY-ONE

'I've got my first date tonight,' Maria excitedly tells me as I arrive at the office.

'Wow, that was quick. Tell me all about it.'

'His name is Declan, he's Irish, three years older than me, works in a bank and very good looking. He joined the dating agency yesterday as well.'

'Sounds like fate. Where are you going?'

'An Italian restaurant in Covent Garden.'

'Well I hope you have a great night and I'll expect a text later to tell me how it all went.'

The timing of Maria's date could not be better. Although I told her yesterday there would be no awkwardness between us after her confession, I was still apprehensive about seeing her this morning but her date with Declan has overcome all of that.

My first day back at work has gone well. Only a handful of colleagues actually knew that I was sacked and then re-instated so in reality it just feels like a normal work day.

Just after three o'clock my mobile rings, it's Karen.

'Danny, Rob's taken Sam when I specifically told him not to only a couple of hours ago,' she sobs.

'Do you know where they are?'

'No, Sam isn't answering his mobile and neither is Rob. He's been so unpredictable lately. I don't know what's he capable of.'

'So he did it out of spite?'

'Yes, absolutely. He did say something about taking Sam to McDonalds or for an ice cream. Belinda's checking the local area right now. I feel helpless.'

'He got to the school before Belinda then?'

'Yeah. The school should always know who is picking him up, but some of the staff are more relaxed about it than others and being Sam's father they obviously thought it was OK for Rob to take him.'

'You really have to nail down that pickup procedure with them.'

'Yes, but right now I need to see my boy.'

'Please don't worry, I'll do my best to find him. I'm leaving now.'

I explain the situation to Frank who immediately tells me to leave and hands me the company credit card, insisting I take a taxi home.

If Belinda is checking the local McDonalds and shops selling ice cream then where do I look? After racking my brain I come up with a possible answer.

'Can you take me to Sainsbury's in Streatham please?' I say to the taxi driver as we approach Brixton.

When we arrive I head straight to the pasta sauce aisle but there's no sign of Sam. I suppose it was a long shot but now I'm concerned. Where the hell are they?

I spot Lewis talking to a customer and rush over to him.

'Sorry to interrupt but by any chance have you seen Sam?'

'Let me finish dealing with this customer,' he replies.

'This is urgent. His father has illegally taken him out of school.'

'I'm sorry. Yes, they're in here somewhere. Let me talk to security,' Lewis replies.

'They're going to look around the back for some Jammie Dodgers for me. There's none out here and it's my favourite biscuit,' the old lady who was talking to Lewis informs me.

I nod and force a smile.

'What's your favourite biscuit? My husband loves Jaffa Cakes but I think they're ghastly.'

'Sorry, I can't think of anything right now.'

'Did I hear you say you were looking for a man and a boy?'

'Yes, that's right.'

'A few minutes ago I saw a man and a boy in the frozen aisle. Maybe that's them?'

'Thanks so much. I also love Jammie Dodgers,' I shout as I dash away. She looks delighted that I agreed with her choice.

In the frozen aisle to my great relief I see Sam and Rob looking at ice cream.

'Just fucking make your mind up. That's the seventh tub you've picked up. Please just decide what you want so we can get out of here,' Rob screams at Sam.

'Are you a complete simpleton?' I say to Rob, who turns, surprised to see me.

'Well look who it is, the only person on this planet who seemingly cannot do no wrong.'

'Did you really think taking Sam out of school, despite Karen telling you not to, was a good idea?'

'When I want advice from someone incapable of fathering a child you'll be top of that list but in the meantime fuck off.'

'I'm taking Sam back to his mother now.'

'Really? I don't think so. I'm his father so you can piss off.'

'I'm going nowhere without Sam.'

'I don't like the mint green one, it makes my head explode,' Sam tells his father.

'Just fucking pick one. How difficult can it be?' Rob shouts back.

'Can we go back to the pasta jars? You didn't let me do any licking.'

'Nothing is ever straight forward with you, is it? Why can't you be normal? Why can't I take you to watch Chelsea without you insisting we leave after five minutes because the noise of the crowd is giving you a headache? Do you know how much those tickets cost? Of course you don't. You don't have a clue about anything, do you? I mean why are you so obsessed with licking things? It's fucking crazy. And when I shut the front door you cry for an hour. What the hell's that about? I can't stand it anymore.'

By this time a small crowd has gathered to watch, including Lewis and a couple of security guards.

Rob stares at me.

'And yes, I did pull his shirt when he was licking the floor and consequently he hit his head on a plinth. Did I do it too aggressively? Yes I did but I didn't intend to hurt him. Let me tell you looking after Sam is a living nightmare but you wouldn't know that cos you haven't got a clue about fatherhood.'

'If you hate your son so much then why do you bother spending time with him?'

'I took him out today with the best intentions, I really did. I wanted to show him a good time but he winds me up and I can't deal with his shit anymore.'

'Well it looks like after this you won't have to because there's going to be repercussions. As for fatherhood I don't think you know the meaning of the word. You really are a useless piece of shit and using Sam to get one over on Karen. Am I right?'

'Yes you are. I know she's a nervous wreck when I'm with her precious son and I can't tell you how much that pleases me. I regret the day I ever fucked her and produced that,' he shouts, pointing at Sam.

I walk towards him until I'm only a few inches away.

'You're a waste of space and if it wasn't for all these people watching I'd beat the fucking shit out of you,' I shout.

He lunges for my throat but I anticipate it and manage to twist his arm behind his back and push him down on the floor. I want to break his arm right now as I twist it further. I want to hurt him badly but the security guards separate us.

Sam walks away from his father and stands next to me.

'My neck is going to hurt again but I want to be with the big feet guy cos I'm fed up getting headaches from your shouting. The big feet guy never shouts at me. He's a quiet man who loves his butter,' Sam tells his father. 'And you're too noisy.'

Rob stares at his son.

'And I don't love you anymore,' Sam adds.

Rob smiles and shakes his head.

A couple of police officers arrive and escort us to an office in the shop to give our accounts of the altercation. When we return to the shop floor one of the officers seems more interested in the cooked chickens than anything else.

'Where's Rob?' I ask him.

'They've taking him down to the station for further questioning. They'll be looking at the CCTV footage for both incidents.'

He then informs me that I'm free to go before making a beeline to the chickens.

'Can I lick the jars now?' Sam asks me.

'Yes you can.'

I ring Karen.

'You can call off the search party, I've found him.'

She starts crying as I explain everything.

'We're coming home and there's something I need to tell you.'

CHAPTER FORTY-TWO

Karen hobbles out to the doorstep to greet us.

'I'm so relieved to see you both, I was so worried.'

'This guy beat the shit out of Dad cos Dad was yelling his brains off at me. I don't want to be with my screaming dad anymore.'

'OK, we'll talk about that later,' Karen says.

'Is the big feet guy walking me to school tomorrow? Aunt Belinda only gave me five pounds and he gave me a tenner yesterday.'

'We'll see...'

'Anyway, I've got to go, I don't want to miss *Tipping Point*.'

'He seems OK considering,' I say to Karen over coffees in the kitchen.

'Yes, but who knows what he's really thinking?'

'I wonder if the police will take any action against Rob?'

'I've no idea. It does seem like an accident even though Rob was heavy-handed. But it puts me in a stronger position if Rob ever tries to take Sam again.'

'How does that make you feel?'

'Today is the first time I've denied Rob access to Sam when he has asked to see him. I think he's mentally unstable right now and until I see evidence he's changed he won't be seeing my boy, I'll make sure of that. But I don't think he's interested. It's a relief.'

'He must be a simpleton. In fact I did call him that earlier,' I say.

'No arguments from me.'

'How could he not know how lucky he was to have you both in his life?'

'Because he's a simpleton?' She smiles.

'Do you ever think back to that first night we met in the pub?' I ask.

'Yes I do and more so recently.'

'What were your first impressions of me?'

'You were shy which I found endearing. I had just broken up with Phil, who confident and brash, a bit like Rob I suppose. You were completely different.'

'So you thought I was a bit of a wuss?'

'No, quite the contrary. After all who was it that asked for your number and actually rang you the next day?'

'Point taken.'

'What did you think of me?' Karen asks.

'You were the most beautiful woman I'd ever seen and as soon as we started talking I fell in love immediately.'

'Wow, it's taken you nineteen years to tell me that?'

'And you know what? I've fallen in love with you all over again. You said the other day it'll be a special person to take on Sam, well I'm not special but I love your son. I feel a need to shield him from this harsh world and I would love to be given the opportunity to do that. Maybe even one day he'll call me by my name?'

Karen shuffles towards me, puts her arms around my neck and kisses me.

'As soon as I saw you again I fell back in love with you. In these last few weeks I've been tormenting myself for ever letting you go through my own stupid mistake. It astonishes me how much love you've shown Sam. He really gave you a hard time initially but for someone with no parental know-how you took it all in your stride and bit by bit you've won him over. In the last week you've been the father he never had and I want you to be with us forever, if that's OK?'

We both start crying, holding each other tightly.

Tears of absolute joy.

CHAPTER FORTY-THREE

As much as I wanted to share a bed with Karen last night we thought it best I slept on the sofa. Sam went through enough trauma yesterday and we didn't want to confuse or upset him.

When I woke up on Christmas Day I felt depressed. Like every other day of the year I would be on my own with little to look forward to. That morning I reflected on the joyous parties Mum and Dad held on Christmas Day for friends and relatives, most of whom are no longer with us. If anything I think Christmas Day is often one of the saddest days of the year for me. Then something magical happened - Karen contacted me. I didn't think it was magical at first but I certainly do now.

Then there was the near fatal hit and run accident which forced me to spend time alone with Sam and later Karen. It created a bond between the three of us. If there had been no accident I would have ended the relationship that day.

It must have been fate.

Karen and I talked until half past three this morning. One hour and twenty-two minutes later Sam woke me up to discuss my views on shoelaces. He doesn't like them as they're too time consuming and prefers the Velcro strap shoes.

I feel shattered but absolutely elated to be back with Karen. I can't quite believe it.

I'm back on the school runs. Belinda was absolutely thrilled with our news. With her brief school run duties now over I'm sure she'll have a healthier bank balance.

'So when are you going back to your Vauxhall house?' Sam asks as we walk to his school.

'Not sure yet. I might stay a bit longer at yours if that's OK?'

'Yeah but Mum still needs a bigger sofa to cover your feet.'

'We'll see.'

I won't tell him just yet that won't be necessary.

'The only people who could hold my hands were Mum and Dad. Sometimes I let Belinda hold my hand but only after I've taken a headache tablet.'

'That's understandable.'

He hands me a piece of paper and a pen.

'What's this?'

'It's an agreement that you can hold my hand as from today. I've crossed out Dad's name and put in yours. Can you sign it please otherwise it's not valid?'

'I'll be delighted to.'

I feel quite emotional signing it as this is a massive step forward in our relationship. I notice that he's written my name as 'big feet guy'. I hand the paper back to him.

'Good, that's looks all in order,' he tells me.

He then takes my hand as we continue to walk.

'Did you ever find out where the cowboys live in America?' I ask.

'They're in loads of places. I created a spreadsheet yesterday with all the cowboy towns and the price of the air fare from Heathrow airport.'

'When you come home this afternoon we'll look at the spreadsheet and the three of us will definitely go to one of those towns very soon. How does that sound?'

He gives me the biggest smile ever, even more joyous than when he's listening to the snap, crackle and pop of his Rice Krispies in the morning. I don't care how much it costs me, it will be worth it just to see him as happy as he is right now.

'Your hand hasn't given me a headache,' he excitedly tells me.

'That's good.'

We then talk about the usual random subjects – pavements, my feet, ants, Custard Creams, Bruce Springsteen and Joe Biden's hair and before I know it we've walked past the infamous mailbox.

'Aren't you going to lick the mailbox today?' I ask Sam.

'Nah, I'm having a day off.'

THE END

Lightning Source UK Ltd.
Milton Keynes UK
UKHW011020220922
409257UK00001B/13

9 781803 812601